Dragon Pox

WRITTEN BY
CAMILLE SMITHSON

ILLUSTRATED BY
SHAREEN HALLIDAY

Text copyright © 2022 by Camille Smithson
Cover Illustrations Copyright © 2022 by Shareen Halliday
Interior Illustrations Copyright © 2022 by Shareen Halliday

Published by Lawley Publishing,
a division of Lawley Enterprises LLC.
All rights reserved.

No part of this publication may be reproduced, or stored in a retrieval system, or transmitted in any form or by any means, electronic, mechanical, photocopying, recording, or otherwise, without written permission of the publisher.

For information regarding permissions, write to:
    Lawley Publishing
    Attention: Permissions Department
    70 S Val Vista Drive #A3 #188
    Gilbert, AZ 85296
    www.LawleyPublishing.com

This book is a work of fiction. Any reference to historical events, real people, or real locales are used as fiction in the work. Other names, characters, places and incidents are all a product of the author's imagination and any resemblance to actual events, locales or people, living or dead is purely coincidental.

Hardcover ISBN   987-1-956357-22-6
Library of Congress Number: 2022933075

For Melanie, Noelle, Oliver, and Preston—my best beta readers, biggest cheerleaders, and favorite science partners.
—*CS*

For my wonderful husband, who finds joy in being my greatest facilitator and has never complained about the cost of art supplies.
—*SH*

Table of Contents

It Started With a Lizard	1
Should That Machine Spark?	11
Are those Wings?	19
Unicorn Promises	27
Rats and Ruckus	35
The Great Hunt	47
And the Secret's Out	55
Racing to Whiplash	63
Dragon Prints in Pink Frosting	71
Flamin' Hots and Dragon Tails	79
The Return of Mr. Muffins	87
Did He Just Speak?	95
Everything Itches	103
Test Tubes and Sticky Goo	111
Dragon Pox	119
Lumps and Scales	129
Fuzzy Note Decoder	137
The Best Deal Ever	147
Mummy Hands	159
Antidote	165
Fizz and Pop	173
Time for the Truth	183
It Ended With a Friend	191

It Started With a Lizard

1

If Hayden's mom caught him sneaking another animal into the house, she'd make him pull weeds for a week. But a lizard had to be better than that stray cat he'd found last time.

He perched on the lowest branch of his favorite apple tree and eyed the puke green lizard with bright purple legs that crept along the smooth limb. The critter crawled right to him, totally fearless, then stopped and flicked out its neon-orange tongue.

Maybe it's hungry? Hayden's stomach growled, reminding him it was almost dinnertime.

He nibbled off a tiny bite of his half-eaten apple and held it out. The lizard inched forward, flicked its awesome tongue, and snatched the slimy chunk off Hayden's fingertip. The green scales along its neck paled as it chewed. The scales flashed fire-engine red in a wavy pattern that raced down the lizard's back before returning to an ugly shade of smashed peas.

Coolest. Thing. Ever.

Yeah. He *needed* the lizard!

If he asked, Mom would just say no. She never said yes to anything fun. She didn't understand—he'd be the most responsible kid in town if she'd just give him a chance. In fact, he'd prove exactly how responsible he was by catching the lizard and taking care of it for a while *before* telling her.

"Come here, little guy." Tossing the apple to the ground, he scooted closer and cupped his hands. The lizard flinched and stared at him, challenging Hayden to make a move.

Challenge accepted.

With wicked fast moves, he snatched the lizard. It squirmed and wrestled against his hold. Angry claws dug into his skin, bringing tiny bubbles of blood and a blaring sting. Hayden gasped. *Stinking razor-sharp claws!* He loosened his hold and then panicked as the slippery beast wiggled free and shot up his arm.

No, no, no!

He scrambled to catch the creature, but it zig-zagged up his skin, scampering under his sleeve. Tiny claws raced over his shoulder and diagonally across his bareback.

Chills skittered across his skin. He twisted, hoping to catch the lizard as it rounded his torso, but he moved too far. His body teetered over the edge of the branch, and air whooshed around him.

Grasping for the tree with both arms, Hayden slammed his weight against the hard bark and wrapped his legs tightly around the limb. All eleven short years of his life flashed before his eyes, and he gaped down at the grass below. Even on the lowest branch, the ground felt more than a mile away. It was always easier to get up the tree than come down.

"Whoa," he released a jagged breath. Yeah, he was done

climbing trees for the day—as soon as he could get his heart to stop racing nine hundred miles per hour. He lowered his feet with another deep breath and mentally counted down from five.

Five. *Please don't die.*

Four. *Or break a leg.*

Th—

The feisty lizard wiggled under his shirt, across his stomach, and straight to his *armpit.*

No!

He released one hand to stop it.

Big mistake.

His other hand slipped, and he crunched against the ground with a heavy thud. Pain tingled down his arms to his hands. He'd definitely feel that for a while. But hey, at least he hadn't hit his head.

He felt around his torso for the mischievous lizard that had almost caused his death. Nothing.

Sitting up, he raked his hands through the cold blades of grass.

"Lizard. Where are you?" he called.

How could his new pet already be lost?

He scanned each and every blade of grass, looking for even a tiny hint of purple. All he found was his sister's useless sock and three decaying apples. Hayden slumped on the ground like a deflated balloon. *So much for raising the best lizard ever.* He leaned back, and his hand squished into a wet pile of mush.

Jerking up, he stared down at the rotting fruit and the apple gunk dripping from his fingers.

"Gross!"

He snatched the sock, wiped the fruit guts on the glittery fabric, and chucked it aside. *Guess the sock was useful, after all.*

When it landed, something moved out from under it.

Ah-ha! Found you.

The lizard shimmied from under the sock and froze in the tall grass, giving him a better look. If only he could get closer without freaking the thing out. Carefully, Hayden twisted to his hands and knees and edged closer.

It was *right there.*

So close, but forever away. If he could just . . .

He reached for its long tail, and his fingers brushed against slick scales. The lizard flinched but didn't run.

Good boy. Just stay right th—.

"Meeeeow!"

An orange tabby cat leaped out of nowhere.

"No!" Hayden scrambled to catch his new pet as it dashed through the grass and disappeared at the edge of the sidewalk. The ball of fur pawed at the lizard's mysterious hiding spot, completely blocking Hayden's view.

"That's *my* lizard." He leaped to his feet and wrapped his arms around the massive cat. The unhappy feline pushed its paws against him, only pausing to watch the lizard reappear and escape in the grass on the other side of the walk.

The cat stopped fighting and glared at Hayden.

Shifting the feline around in his arms, he held the heavy beast up until they were face to face. "Now, look what you've done."

The little devil licked its chomps and stared back with annoyance.

Hayden scowled. "Oh no! You're not eating my pet." He secured the cat against him and tiptoed to where his lizard had disappeared. *There'd be no lizard catching with this hungry cat on the loose.*

"We better get you home."

Only, where was home? Hayden knew all the animals in the neighborhood, and this giant tabby wasn't one of them. He ran a finger under the cat's thin black collar until he found its name tag. The words "Mr. Muffins" were engraved in tiny print.

"Mr. Muffins, huh?" He chuckled. "Bet someone was hungry when they named you."

The cat narrowed his eyes and scrunched his nose, exposing angry fangs.

Every muscle in Hayden's body tensed. "I mean, it's a great name."

Mr. Muffins stared a moment longer, then sneezed gunk all over his face.

"Yuck!" he said, wiping the cat snot onto his sleeve.

He scanned the street. New neighbors had moved into the old Anderson place a couple of days ago. He'd heard Dad whispering to Mom over breakfast about the big moving truck that showed up in the middle of the night. They moved everything into the house in the dark, not even using a flashlight. Dad found the whole thing suspicious. Mom said they must be quiet people and planned to bake them cookies.

Hayden stroked the soft fur around the cat's ears. "Did you move in next door?"

Mr. Muffins mewed.

Like a cat would answer. Still, there was only one way to find out.

Cutting across his side of the yard, he marched closer to the familiar large brown barn that had sat vacant since before his family moved to Timberline. Paint peeled off the old wood, and the shutters dangled, making the barn look haunted. Of course, that never stopped him from sneaking through the window to explore.

But today, everything looked different. Instead of barred up,

the huge door stood open, like a big yawning mouth. A small black bike leaned against the worn wood. *So, your owner is a kid?* Another kid with a pet.

He hugged Mr. Muffins a smidgen tighter. The cat's long soft fur tickled at his neck, reminding him of how great it would be to have a snuggly friend.

It was so frustrating. Here he lived in a farming town, and he was the *only* kid without a pet. *So not fair!* But he'd solve that problem—as soon as he returned Mr. Muffins, he'd find his lizard.

He started past the barn when a flicker of light caught his eye. *What was that?* Creeping toward the door, he peered into the black cavern, but all he could see was thick, cold fog. A spooky shiver tiptoed up his back. The old barn had never felt so *creepy* before. And so awesome.

Just take the cat home.

Except . . . *what was that bubbling, sizzling noise?*

He *had* to check it out. Holding Mr. Muffins as his personal protection shield, he crept past the door and into the fog. It wasn't that he was scared—not one bit. It was just, having someone with him made him braver.

Something gurgled and boiled in the dark. Then, everything was quiet, until . . .

A loud crackle pierced the air like a bolt of electricity.

Hayden's heart nearly leaped out of his chest, and he jumped back.

Mr. Muffins let off a long hiss and jerked sideways, his sharp claws climbing up Hayden's body.

"Shh. It's okay." Hayden said, fighting to protect and comfort the startled cat. "It's just . . ." *What? A bolt of lightning?*

Mr. Muffins wouldn't have it and leaped into the shadowed room.

"Hello? Mr. Muffins?" Hayden whispered, not sure if he

should chase after the crazy cat or just go.

Probably just go.

If he left now, he still had time to find his lizard before dinner. Backing out of the barn, he stumbled on something in the dark.

Gurgle. Gulp. Glug. Burp.

The noise grew louder, and his heart pounded harder.

As Hayden stood, a spark of electricity flicked in the corner of the room, then arced and snapped.

Whoa! What was that?

Should That Machine Spark?

2

Lightning sliced through the fog, illuminating the back corner of the barn. Hayden rubbed his eyes. There was no way this was real.

Electricity arced between two gigantic tubes that bubbled with green and yellow liquid, like giant lava lamps. And between them, weirdest of all, sat a mysterious old furnace. It looked just like the one his grandfather used to have—like a beat-up, lifeless old droid from a *Star Wars* movie—but Grandpa's never glowed purple like *that*.

The arc disappeared, and Hayden blinked several times against the sudden darkness. Streaks of light had burned into his eyes, making it look like a bolt of lightning still flashed behind his eyelids. He couldn't leave now, not until he got a better look at whatever *that* was. He could always find another lizard.

Inching closer, he reached his hand into the cold blackness. Behind him, the sunlight stopped at the doorway as if even it was too afraid to sneak inside.

Maybe he shouldn't either. Without Mr. Muffins, he was trespassing.

Gulp. Gurgle. Burp.

The bubbling machine restarted its song. One quick look, and he was out of there. Through the fog, the dim purple light flickered, and a low hum started. A small dark shadow cut into the purple light, like a tooth on a jack-o-lantern. Something was *in* there.

He stepped closer. And closer. His heart began pounding hard against his chest, making him want to run. Instead, he ignored it, ducked lower, and shuffled faster.

The bubbling grew louder and louder and louder—then stopped.

The moment he reached the machine, lightning sparked all around him. Hayden dove to the floor to get himself as far away from the arcing electricity as possible and pinched his eyes closed. His heart gave up trying to escape out of his chest and instead tried leaping out his throat.

The buzz lasted well past five-Mississippi seconds, and then, just as suddenly as it came, the room was black.

Dragon Pox

I almost died. I almost died.

Why would his new neighbors have an electricity machine in their barn anyhow?

Hayden rolled onto his back. Above him, a faint mystical light continued to glow.

Now or never. Who knew when the electric light show would repeat, and him having a major freak-out session wouldn't help. He inched up the furnace, crouching eye-level with the glowing light that shone through the wide opening.

Just inside the furnace's angry mouth lay a single blue egg laying on a bed of straw. The thing was slightly larger than one from a chicken, with large dark spots dotting the shell. *What kind of creature was in there?*

The egg twitched, then jerked slightly one way and then the other. *Was it . . . hatching?*

Here he had a front-row seat.

He scooted closer, now only inches from the rusty machine, and slid a hand under the lamp. In the purple glow, his skin turned a shade of neon blue. *Cool.*

Wait. What if the purple light was radioactive? Would he lose a finger? Or grow an extra one? He wiggled his fingers around—a sly grin curving at his lips. Having an extra might come in handy.

Behind him, something brushed across the concrete floor. In one quick move, he ripped his hand from the light and ducked down, waiting. Nothing happened.

It was probably Mr. Muffins.

Just another peek. Just until it hatches. The egg continued to twitch under the glowing purple light, and Hayden watched it, trying to ignore the nervous shaking of his hands.

A heavy weight slammed against the concrete and closed the big barn door.

The hairs on Hayden's arms stood on end. No way that was Mr. Muffins. He needed to get out of there.

But the egg was hatching! He'd miss the whole thing.

"Hey. You shouldn't be in here," a low gravelly voice called from the darkness.

Hayden froze. Time was up. The man was right. He *should* leave. But his feet wouldn't listen, not when he was so close to seeing the egg hatch.

Gulp. Gurgle. Glump.

The purple light flickered, and new noise started—like the

hose on a vacuum cleaner. Air rushed past his face into the furnace.

The egg rocked back, then slid through the straw toward a dark hole. The machine planned to *eat* it. No way he'd let that happen! Hayden reached out and scooped it up. He'd leave alright, but he was saving whatever was inside there first.

Moving as carefully as possible, he slid the egg under his shirt. The shell burned where it rubbed against his skin, but he forced himself not to flinch. If the stranger could see him, he wouldn't give himself away.

"It's okay, little buddy. I'll keep you safe," he whispered, "and warm."

The bright beam of a flashlight pinned his feet to the ground. Hayden couldn't see whoever stood at the other end of the light, but the flashlight-wielding stranger could definitely see him.

Panic climbed up his throat. *Step one: get home.* Who was he kidding? Step one was the *only* step. He was too scared to come up with any other plans.

"Come on out now," the man said. "Didn't your mom teach you not to snoop in other people's barns?"

Hayden's brain screamed at him to run—fast—but the beam of light superglued him in place. His stomach flipped upside down and back again. Sweat ran down his waist where the hot egg pressed against his flesh.

"What's your name, boy?"

"Hay . . . Hayden," he stammered.

"Huh. Hayden. See anything interesting?" The man's question boomed around the room.

How could he *not* see anything interesting? He'd seen something. Hayden knew it. The man knew it. Lying would only prolong his agony.

"I . . . I saw that." Behind him, the machine bubbled. "I only came in for a closer look. Promise."

If only he could see the man's face. Was he mad? He'd come clean about everything else—just not now. Dad always said a little dirt didn't hurt.

The bubbling stopped, and the room grew quiet. *That meant . . .* Hayden looked back at the machine.

Zip. Zap. Zip.

Sparks flickered. Electricity blasted through the air. No way he would stay here under an electrical storm. Hayden clung to the lump in his shirt and bolted to the door.

As he closed the distance between him and the man at the door, the flashlight flicked off. Something on the machine popped and crunched, and a bright light blazed behind him. Hayden peeked back and gasped. Small flames burned the straw inside the furnace—exactly where the egg had been.

"What in the world?" The man raced toward the machine. As he slipped past, Hayden caught a glimpse of his face. Not his entire face, but enough to see the enormous green blister at the end of his chin.

Was that real?

Probably not. His eyes were playing tricks on him. Still, he didn't plan to stick around and find out.

He rushed outside—the sudden brightness of the sun blinded him, but that didn't stop him. He sprinted across the gravel road, away from the weird barn and its creepy owner. The faster he could get away, the better.

He ran hard, and the egg twitched even harder.

Are those Wings?

3

Hayden eased the heavy front door open and panicked at the low moan of the hinges. *Had Mom heard that?*

No dishes clinking in the kitchen ... no footsteps thumping from the bedrooms ... all clear.

Slipping inside, he pushed the door closed, cringing as the annoying thing released a long, deep *creeeak*.

"Hayden? Is that you?" Mom called from the kitchen.

Scrud!

The egg, still pressed against his stomach, twitched frantically. Even though it waited at the top of the stairs, his room might as well have been on the other side of the planet. *Could I make it without getting caught?* If Mom found him bringing another pet into the house, he would be doomed to a never-ending lecture and hours of weeding—or worse ... he might miss Halloween fun next week.

The egg danced against his skin. It was time for action. He couldn't exactly sneak the thing back into the creepy neighbor's barn.

He would have to go into stealth ninja mode. Then, maybe Mom would think she heard something and go on doing Mom-stuff. He crept to the base of the stairs and climbed them one by one, making sure to avoid the spots that always squeaked.

"Hayden?" The light click-clacking of Mom's shoes on the tile made his heart hiccup.

"Yes?" he squeaked in a voice a half octave too high. Clearing his throat, he tried again for nonchalance. "It's me. I'm just going to my room to . . . um . . . hang out." Forget stealth mode—he raced up the rest of the stairs.

"Don't forget, you have a few chores you still need to finish up," Mom said, her voice growing as she came into view.

He shielded the lump in this shirt the best he could and gave her a thumbs up. "Yep. I'm totally on it in just a few minutes."

She folded her arms, a single brow raised. "Ten minutes tops."

"Thanks, Mom." Hayden flew through his door so fast, the words barely made it out before it slammed shut behind him. If only he could lock it to keep himself safe for a few minutes.

Or maybe . . .

With his free hand, he dumped the dirty clothes from his laundry basket in front of the door. There—a barrier.

He lowered to his knees and uncovered the egg, laying it on the shaggy brown carpet. It jolted and wiggled in a small circle.

This was really happening. A ghost of a line spread across the shell. Hayden slapped a hand over his mouth to hold back the scream of excitement that threatened to escape.

Ideas of what hid inside paraded through his mind. A lizard? No, the egg was too big for a lizard. Unless it was an alligator.

He froze. *Could he have just brought an alligator inside his house?*

That would be sweet! But Mom would never let him keep a baby alligator. She'd think it would eat the family up or something.

Maybe it was a turtle. Or a platypus! *What did platypus eggs look like anyhow?*

Whatever it was, he'd keep his pet safe and prove to Mom he could handle the responsibility.

Just please don't let it be an alligator.

The egg started rolling across the lumpy carpet.

"Oh no, you don't," he said, placing a hand in its path.

Scrape. Scratch. Crunch.

A single claw poked through the egg. Hayden jerked his hand away. Pieces of eggshell chipped and crumbled to the carpet as the hole grew. Another claw burst through the shell.

The sunlight from his window bounded off what looked like dark scaly skin.

A lizard! Not just any lizard. This one had midnight blue scales and light purple talons. *Way cool.* Much better than the lizard from the tree. Excitement bubbled and popped in Hayden's stomach.

Finally, the remainder of the egg shattered, exposing spikes and—*wings?*

Impossible.

The creature stretched its spiny purple wings and flapped once. Teal swirls raced over and around its blue scales in what looked like dragon racing stripes.

He'd found a dragon.

A dragon!

He let out a loud whoop. *Oops!* Too loud. Mom would find

out! Buttoning his lips, he did his ultimate, *silent* victory dance. *Dragons were real? When did that happen?*

And he had one.

In his room.

From tallest spike to smallest toe, the dragon wasn't any bigger than a kitten—the perfect hiding size.

Until it grew.

Wait! How big did dragons get? Would this guy be the size of a house cat or a lion? And how fast? Would it outgrow the bedroom before he had time to train it?

He skirted around it, trying to get a better look. The stubborn dragon refused to hold still, turning its head as Hayden moved and making it impossible for him to see.

"Hold still!"

The dragon twisted its head again, following his move. That's when the realization hit—it was playing with him.

Hayden moved to the left. The dragon followed, swaying in

that direction. Its black eyes locked onto his, then blinked once.

He inched closer, holding out his palm. The trick worked for dogs. Perhaps it would work with dragons, too.

"Come here, little buddy. It's okay," he whispered. Little Buddy was a ridiculous dragon name. He'd think up something better.

Nightshade? With dark scales and the swirls, that might work. No. The name still didn't feel right. It sounded more like something his sister, Makayla, would name one of her unicorns.

The dragon looked at his palm, then up. Slowly, it stepped out from the crumble of eggshell dust, wobbled slightly on the uneven ground, and caught itself. Tiny shell pieces dropped to the carpet as it took another step toward Hayden.

"Keep coming. You got this."

Instead of taking another step, it lowered to all four feet, lifted its long thin tail in the air, wiggled the tail a few times, and prepared to pounce.

This should be fun. Maybe he could name the dragon Pouncer? No, that sounded too much like one of those magical reindeer.

Hayden mirrored his new friend, putting his face to the ground and rear in the air, and waited.

One-Mississippi . . .

Two-Mississippi . . .

The dragon sprang into the air with its wings spread, and it flapped. Hayden shot up. *Was it flying?*

With two uncoordinated flaps, it flopped to the ground, front feet hitting the carpet before its back, sending the critter into a sloppy somersault. Well, more like a half somersault. With all four legs in the air, it looked like it was playing dead.

Hayden laughed and carefully ran a finger along its silky

stomach. The dragon squirmed and wiggled, whipping its long tail back and forth. It opened its mouth and let out a squeak.

Do dragons laugh?

He couldn't help himself—he had to tickle it again. A broad smile crossed the dragon's face. It squirmed faster and gripped his finger with its claws as if to make him stop.

"Do you like to be tickled?"

Squawk. Cluck. Mew.

"I'll take that as a yes."

He moved closer and tickled it again. This time when the dragon squirmed, its long tail whipped into Hayden's bare knee, slicing his skin.

"Ouch," he hissed, shifting to get a better look at his leg. An angry red stripe stared back at him. Man, he'd been hit good. He lifted his hand to rub the stinging skin, but the dragon clung to his finger. The long tail wrapped around his wrist like a tight rope.

A whipping-rope.

Hayden trailed the tip of his finger along the scaly tail. He didn't want to get on the bad end of this whip if it ever lashed out.

That's it. The perfect name.

"Whiplash!"

Whiplash opened his mouth in a dragon smile and crawled around Hayden's hand until he rested on his arm. A long, neon blue tongue flicked from between dragon lips, tickling several strands of his arm hair.

"Whoa." Seriously, could this dragon be any cooler? "Are you hungry?"

New babies were always hungry, weren't they? Careful not to shake him too much, Hayden stood and walked to his desk.

What did dragons eat? He rummaged through the contents of his top drawer. A sock? No. Stapler? Definitely not. The rest of the sugar cookie he snuck this morning? He shrugged. *Who didn't like cookies?*

He shuffled around the annoying old homework littering his floor to get to his bed. Peeling the dragon from his arm, he set him on the dark blue galactic bedspread. The moment Whiplash touched the blanket, his swirl of teal disappeared, blending seamlessly with this midnight blue scales. Wow. *That'll make it easy to hide you.*

Hayden broke off a chunk of cookie and tossed it on the bed. Whiplash squealed, circling the treat and flicking his long tongue. One clawed foot grasped the large crumb—then he shoved the whole thing into his mouth. He wagged his tail and panted like an over-eager puppy. Hayden chuckled and threw another piece.

This time, Whiplash caught it in his mouth, swallowing it whole.

Hayden snapped off another piece and rested it on his open palm. Whiplash snaked toward him along the star-printed blanket. Tiny talons tickled his fingers as the dragon scampered onto his skin. He slowly raised his hand and nestled it against his chest. Whiplash rubbed the top of his silky head against Hayden's hand and clucked.

Dragons cluck? Well, this one did.

Whiplash flipped onto his back, exposing his smooth stomach, and clucked again. Hayden pulled him even closer—into the softest hug he could give.

"If *cluck* means 'I love you,' then I cluck you, too."

Footsteps thumped next to the closed door. His ten minutes were up. The knob turned, but the door caught on the pile of clothes. Hayden's stomach crunched into a ball. He scanned his room, looking for a place to hide his new pet.

Scrud! Nothing.

Wait! He turned and looked back at his comforter. *Camouflage bedspread it is!* Hayden dropped onto the bed, shoving Whiplash behind him—just as the door pushed over his gym shorts and swung open.

Unicorn Promises

4

"Whatcha hiding?" Makayla asked in a high-pitched, whiny voice. Even though she was two years younger, she sometimes acted more like his mother.

"Nothing," Hayden said, shifting his weight. Whiplash scampered along his arm. He leaned to his elbow to block the dragon from her view.

She squinted at him. "Sure, nothing. That's why you jumped onto your bed the second I opened the door. And what's up with the booby-trap?" Stepping closer, she craned her head to look around him.

He blocked her with his free hand. "I was just . . . hanging out." His gabby sister would never keep a secret from Mom. Secrets slipped through her lips like a bucket with a hole—dripping a trail everywhere she went.

"Hanging out?" She stopped straining and stared at him, a question mark on her brow. "In your room? Why?" Her lips formed a big 'O', and then her face softened. "Did you get grounded?"

He scowled at her. *Of course, she'd assume the worst.* "No. I just . . . needed a break."

Whiplash batted at the back of his arm with sharp claws. Hayden wrapped his fingers around whatever part of the dragon he could grab without making a scene and willed his sister to leave.

She didn't.

Instead, she stood there, arms crossed, all sassy.

"Well, Mom told me to come get you. She's—"

A raspy growl interrupted Makayla's sentence, and her jaw dropped for a second before she stepped closer. "Did you adopt another stray cat? Mom's going to ground you until you're twelve."

"No," he barked. "I promised not to take in any other cats after Tiger."

Tiger. What a mistake he'd been. Hayden gave him fresh milk, and what'd he get in return? Shredded curtains and a two-week grounding—not to mention all the weeding. Thank heavens Dad took pity and helped.

"I heard a cat. I know you're lying," Makayla said, her voice rising. She charged him, but he caught her just in time, not that it stopped her from wrestling against him. His grip on his sister tightened as he fought to keep a hold on his dragon with his other hand.

"I'm not ly—" Pain sparked his wrist. He instantly released both hands, bringing his throbbing wrist to his mouth. Whiplash squawk-hissed and slithered around the bedspread.

Makayla released the scream of all screams—the kind that shatters glass or alerts your mother to a mass murderer. He dove at his sister, covering her mouth with one hand and bracing her with the other.

"Shh—You'll make Mom come." She choked down her scream but kept shoving at him. He needed her to understand—to see things his way. "Please. Mom won't ever let me have a pet until I prove I can handle it. If you tattle on me now, I'll never have a chance."

She stilled.

"I'm going to let you go," he said. "Just promise you won't scream."

She nodded. He loosened his grip. *Please don't scream. Please don't scream.* He clenched his teeth and peeled his hand from her lips.

Silence.

"Makayla, Hayden, what's going on?" Mom's voice called from somewhere downstairs. Their eyes locked, and Hayden knew this was the end.

Makayla walked to the door, rested a hand on the frame, and glanced back at him. Then she leaned into the hall. He closed his eyes, preparing for the worst.

"It was my fault, Mom," she said. "Everything's okay."

His eyes flew open in shock as his sister closed the door and stepped toward him. Whiplash slithered around her feet and clucked.

After that save, I 'cluck' her, too.

"What *is* that thing?" she asked, jumping to the side.

"I think he's a dragon." Hayden scooped Whiplash off the ground and held him out so she could get a better view.

"Where did you—? How can it—?" Her words fell out of her mouth in a jumbled mess. She swallowed and gave him a hard stare. "I want a unicorn."

"A unicorn?" *Had she lost her mind?*

"Yes. With pink hair and glitter," she added, without a hint of humor.

Hayden pulled Whiplash away from his sister. "What, do I look like a sorcerer to you?"

She placed her hands on her hips and shook her head. "I don't know what magic you did to get a dragon here but use it to make me a unicorn."

He smirked at her insane notion. "I didn't make a dragon. I hatched him." Whiplash crawled up his arm, tickling his skin as he circled around to the underside. Remembering the disastrous adventure with the last lizard in his armpit, he moved Whiplash up to perch on his shoulder.

"It's beautiful. Can you hatch me one?" She moved closer to Hayden, her foot pushing against his. He ignored the encroachment, letting her pet Whiplash's head and under his chin. She tickled the soft flesh under his neck, and he wiggled and giggled at her touch.

"Probably not," he said, wondering how much he should tell her. "I found the egg by accident." In the barn. Next door. Did that mean the egg, or now the dragon, was the neighbors?

No. If it weren't for him, the egg would have been sucked into that awful machine. Or worse—burnt to a crisp. He'd rescued it.

"By accident, where?"

Should he be honest? Or tell a white lie? *Mom always goes on about trust and truth.* Hayden cringed at the traitorous mental reminder. *Mom also never lets him do anything fun.*

Makayla ran a finger along the end of Whiplash's spikes. Having someone to share his secret with was *definitely* more fun than hiding it. *If* she didn't gab.

"You have to promise you won't tell—about any of it. The dragon. The egg. Anything." What was he thinking? She'd probably tell the first person she ran into as soon as they left his room.

She didn't tell Mom a few minutes ago.

"I promise," she said, not moving her attention from the creature on his shoulder.

"I mean it, Makayla," he said in his most stern voice.

Her hand dropped, and she stepped back from him. "I said, I *promise.*"

"How do I know you won't gab to Mom or your friends?"

The more he thought about it, the more he was certain he *shouldn't* tell her. Not with so much on the line. Though . . . it wasn't like she could unsee a dragon.

"I know!" She bounced on her feet as the words burst from her mouth. "I can swear on my book of unicorns. I watched a movie with Dad where everyone swore on a book, and they *had* to tell the truth."

"Your unicorn book?"

"Sure, it's thick. You'll see." She dashed out the door, leaving it wide open for the world while she acted out her crazy plan. It made sense, though. He'd also seen enough of Dad's favorite law shows to know what she meant. Yeah, it was perfect.

She skipped back into his room with her *Big Book of Unicorns* ready in hand. Hayden hurried to close the door behind her.

"Okay. Fine." He pulled the sparkling encyclopedia of all things rainbows and unicorns and plopped it on his dresser. "Put your left hand on the book and your right in the air. Then, repeat after me."

She stepped over to the bed and rested her left hand on the cover. Raising her right, she gave a sharp nod.

"Ready."

Whiplash crept to Hayden's neck and flicked his tongue in Hayden's ear, sending a wave of wiggles down his spine. Apparently, the dragon was ready, too. Hayden moved him back to his shoulder and away from his ear.

"Say 'I, Makayla, promise I will not tell anyone about my brother's dragon or the egg that hatched it, or . . .'" *What would be a good threat?* The mess of papers and clothes on the floor caught his attention. *Perfect.* "'. . . I will do his chores for a year.'"

She hesitated, her gaze landing on the dragon. After a deep breath, she shook her head.

"I, Makayla, promise not to tell anyone about your dragon or its egg." She stopped.

Hayden waited. When she didn't continue, he glared at her. "Or you'll do my chores for a year. You can't forget that part. It could be worse. I didn't say you'd have to give up all your unicorn posters."

Makayla rolled her eyes. "Fine. Or I'll do your chores for a year." She pushed the book aside. "Now, where'd you find the egg?"

"Remember, you promised, no telling," he said, the knot in his stomach releasing. "I was in the yard doing *stuff* when I found this strange tabby cat stalking around. I figured he must belong to the people that just moved in." He hesitated for a moment, stroking Whiplash's head for courage.

"So, I took the cat home. And when I reached the old barn, there was this buzzing zapping noise."

"Like a mosquito zapper?" she asked.

A mosquito zapper times a million. "I don't know what it was, but sparks were flying everywhere from this weird machine, and right there in the middle of it was the strangest spotted egg."

Makayla held up a hand. "Wait. The egg was in the old Anderson's barn, in the neighbor's machine, and you took it?" She looked shocked. Of course, she'd assume he stole it.

"It wasn't stealing. I *rescued* it. I only wanted to watch it hatch, but then the machine started sucking air into it like an evil, hungry vacuum cleaner. After I grabbed it, the whole thing started on fire. If I hadn't saved it, this guy would have been all burnt up."

She gasped. "How scary—poor thing." She put a hand out for Whiplash. He flicked his tongue at her. When she didn't twitch, he slowly climbed onto her palm.

"She needs a name," said Makayla.

Hayden did a double-take.

"She? It's a boy dragon."

"Whatever." She raised the dragon up on her pointer finger. His tiny claws gripped around it as if it were a twig. "How about Nighty, because he's so dark. Or Swirls, like the design on his back."

"His name is Whiplash."

The dragon flicked his tail in the air in agreement.

"That's a great name," she said, petting Whiplash across his back. His tail began to wag back and forth. "So, what do you plan to do with him when you go to school tomorrow?"

School? How'd he overlooked that obstacle? There was nowhere he could leave his new pet in his room, not when he hadn't had a chance to make him a real habitat. Mom would definitely find him. Plus, he didn't want to leave him.

Then what was the alternative?

Take the little guy to school? He could keep him safe and play with him whenever he wanted.

Hayden grinned at his sister. "I'm going to bring him with me."

Rats and Ruckus

5

The first bell rang at Timberline Elementary. Hayden rubbed the sweat from his hands and peeled his backpack open. The temporary shoebox habitat he'd made last night hid inside, still intact after the bike ride to school.

His plan was working. Now all he had to do was beat the rest of his class inside and stash it in his desk.

Kids raced past him—all in so much of a rush to get to their lines that they ignored him completely. Perfect. He slipped the lid off the box, just to peek. Whiplash was asleep, nuzzled up next to yesterday's stinky old gym sock. So far, so good. The medicine cup that held water lay on its side next to a wet spot of cardboard.

Moving quickly, he propped the cup up against the corners of the box, then refilled it from his water bottle.

He glanced up. The playground had become a ghost town. *Oops!*

Makayla was lined up with the rest of the third graders,

watching him. She hadn't spilled the beans to Mom about his new pet, so that was good. But she *had* lectured him the entire bike ride about how ridiculous he was for bringing a dragon to school.

He turned away, trying to ignore her nervous looks, and zipped up his backpack. If she'd had her way, Whiplash would still be home, and he'd be spending the whole day freaking out over whether or not his dragon was safe—and hidden from Mom.

This way, he could check on him whenever he wanted *and* play with him at recess.

Trying not to jostle his bag too much, Hayden jogged to the end of Mrs. Bowers' fifth-grade line just as it disappeared past the large glass doors.

He fumbled his way to the cubby closet with the rest of the class and hung up his backpack. His stomach squirmed like a fish stuck in a glass bowl. How was he supposed to move Whiplash's box to his desk without anyone noticing? Everyone was in the classroom, and Mrs. Bowers was getting things started. If only he'd kept to his plan and come inside before everyone else.

He slid back the zipper and peeked inside again. Whiplash snored softly and rolled over, kneading the sock with sharp claws.

What if he wakes up hungry?

Maybe leaving him a snack would help. Hayden cracked open his lunch box—all the typical stuff. A sandwich, some grapes, and—oh, Mom had left him a brownie. *Nice.* He plucked two plump grapes off the vine and laid them next to his sleeping friend. *Whiplash might like a morning treat, too.* Heck, if Hayden had his pick, he'd eat the brownie for *breakfast*. Breaking off a chocolatey chunk of goodness, he put a piece in the box and

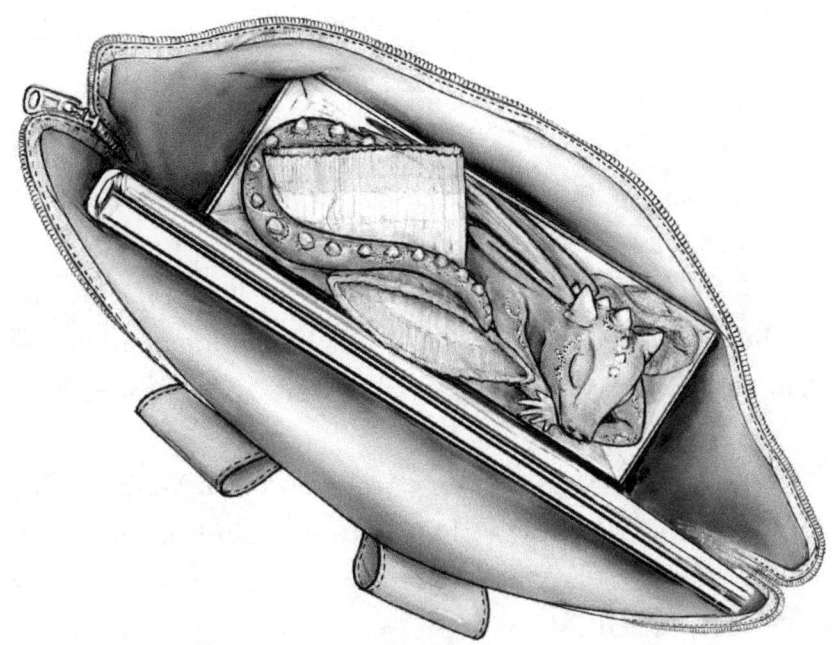

shoved the rest in his mouth.

"Hayden," said Mrs. Bowers from the front of the classroom. "This is not lunchtime. I need you to put the food back in your lunch box and have a seat."

Scrud! His cheeks burned, and he tried to ignore everyone staring at him. He wiped stray crumbs from his lips and acted natural. From the far side of the room, Evan whispered something to Levi. Both boys snickered.

Great. So much for playing it cool.

He zipped up his pack and shoved his lunch box into the class bin.

"Sorry, Mrs. Bowers," he muttered as he plopped into his seat next to Seth.

With a killer fauxhawk and wicked basketball skills, Seth was the most popular kid in the class. Hayden tried to pull off the fauxhawk before, but it flopped to one side like one of those whales with a curly fin.

At least Seth was chill and didn't seem to care about being the best.

Plus, having a dragon was way better than any fauxhawk. Not that Hayden was in a competition with him or anything.

He pulled out his planner and a pencil and tried to focus on the day's agenda. Fat chance that would happen—not with Whiplash hiding in his bag.

Man, today was going to drag.

"Excuse me, Mrs. Bowers," said Principal Whittle, gliding into the room. A short girl shadowed behind her in all black clothes and long dark hair covering half of her face. She could have *literally* been a shadow if it weren't for her ghostly white skin.

"Students, this is Brooklyn Slade." Principal Whittle sidestepped, putting all the attention on the shy, awkward girl.

Brooklyn seemed more interested in her pair of heavy black boots than the class, and Hayden didn't blame her. He'd been the new kid once, back in second grade, and he could go his whole life without ever being in that situation again.

"Brooklyn's dad is the new science teacher at the middle school, so some of you might have him next year." A huge smile stretched across Principal Whittle's face. "Isn't that exciting?" She must have thought somehow this information would help the new girl's chances of surviving fifth grade. "I hope you help her feel welcome."

Yeah, right.

The first semester was half over, and everyone already had their cliques. But then, a girl as pretty as she probably didn't have any problems making friends.

"Hello, Brooklyn. Why don't you take a seat over here," Mrs.

Bowers said, gesturing at the empty desk across from Hayden. Brooklyn slid into the plastic seat and shot him an embarrassed smile.

He gulped and smiled back. At least he hoped what his face was doing looked like a smile.

"Alright, everyone. It's time for independent reading," said Mrs. Bowers as she closed the door behind Principal Whittle and headed back to her desk.

The room erupted into sounds of shuffling and knocking as everyone pulled out their books. Hayden rifled through the bin in his desk, searching for the latest edition of the *National Geographic: Kids Mission* series that he'd started the day before. Gone. He glanced around the room. Everyone else was already reading.

No, almost everyone. Evan smirked over *The Diary of a Wimpy Kid*.

Those punks always messed with his desk. One of these days, he'd get them back with the ultimate prank—but he'd have to think of one first.

Ugh! Even the new girl had a book. Or . . . was that a *science textbook?* He couldn't read the title, but the cover clearly had a microscope and a beaker with pink liquid. That was *different.* Guess her dad would be proud, being a science geek and all.

"Hayden, have you misplaced your book?" Mrs. Bowers asked.

He glared at Evan for getting him in trouble. *Again.* "I think I loaned mine to Evan or something."

Evan chuckled and gave Levi a low five over their desks.

"Well," she said with an exaggerated swoop of her hand. "Go pick out a book from the community library." Yep, she was annoyed.

Hayden threw his pencil onto his desk and took the walk of shame to the bookshelf in the corner next to the backpack cubby. He scanned the covers on the top shelf, avoiding anything pink and sparkly. Mrs. Bowers kept all the babyish books on *that* shelf. They were in fifth grade. He wouldn't be caught dead reading a book with a puppy on the cover, no matter how fluffy its ears looked. That'd be like putting a target on his back and asking kids to take shots at him.

Plucking a dragon book off the second shelf, he thumbed through the pages. *This looked promising.* Maybe he'd even learn something about training a dragon, like the title indicated.

"Please take the book back to your seat," Mrs. Bowers said in the voice she saved for when she was frustrated but trying to cover it up with a weird English accent. It didn't fool anyone, but at least she wasn't yelling.

He twisted the book in his hands and started back to his seat. *Scratch. Scratch. Ruffle. Scratch.*

He paused. *Was that?* No. Couldn't be. The cracked book made for a great shield. He could pretend to read and inch closer to Whiplash at the same time. He moved closer to the rows of hanging bags. The noise stopped. He waited, straining to hear any sounds.

Scratch.

His eyes shot to his backpack, teetering on the hook. It bounced and wobbled. Hayden gawked. *Whiplash!*

Mrs. Bowers cleared her throat. Hayden peeked over the top of the book to see her gesture to his seat with her eyes.

But his dragon. The small scratching sounds itched at his nerves as he returned to his desk and sank into his seat. *Could anyone else hear it?* Opening his book to a random page, he hid his face again and watched the ticking time bomb that he'd left in his backpack. *Oh, please don't let anyone else notice.*

"Your book's upside down," Brooklyn whispered over her own.

Hayden focused on the words on the page—yep, upside down—then flipped it right side up.

"Thanks," he whispered. She shrugged and went back to reading.

Cluck. Squeak.

Several books lowered. Other kids started to look over at the cubby.

Please stop.

He could fake sick and take Whiplash home. *Yeah. That's what he'd do.* He forced a cough.

Brooklyn fixed him with a suspicious stare.

Okay, not convincing enough. He lowered himself in his chair and held his stomach with a moan.

From the corner of his eye, he saw Mrs. Bowers sit up, her attention a hundred and fifty percent on the cubby.

Scratch. Scratch.

Mrs. Bowers rose slowly. "Does anyone hear that?" she asked.

Hayden's arm shot up. "Mrs. Bowers, I have a—"

YOOOWWWL!

Several boys jumped out of their seats and rushed to the cubby. No way Hayden was going to let them get to his dragon first. He blasted out of his chair, letting it crash to the ground behind him, and shoved his way through.

"Boys, stay back!" Mrs. Bowers pushed her way between the boys and the backpacks.

The noise stopped. All Hayden could hear was the sound of his heart thumping—double time.

Mrs. Bowers hovered by the cubby with an arm stretched out like a human barricade against over-anxious boys. Her other hand was fisted at her mouth, holding her screams in. The moment ticked on for what felt like an hour. Then Evan and Levi began scratching against their desks and laughing.

"Hilarious, boys," she said, her shoulders raising up to her ears. "Playtime is over." She pinched her lips together in a tight knot, and she studied the now quiet scene.

Evan slouched in his seat, his freckled face shining red with amusement. The other boys stumbled back to their desks, leaving Hayden and Mrs. Bowers alone.

Now was his chance. He held his stomach. "Mrs. Bowers, I have a stomachache. I need to go home."

She chuckled sarcastically. "Your stomach wasn't hurting too bad when you chucked your chair and ran across the room."

Oops. Dread crept up his throat like vomit. Maybe he really was sick. He clutched his stomach tighter.

She shook her head. "Go back to your seat, and we'll see how you feel in a bit."

He dragged his feet back to his desk. *How could he convince her he really was sick?*

Thump! Bam!

Mrs. Bowers screamed.

Hayden spun, forgetting to clutch his stomach. His gaze shot to the cubby—to his bag where he left Whiplash. Only, his backpack wasn't there.

Where was it?

He ran to the closet—him and everyone else. Several bags lay on the floor. His backpack twitched and bounced in the middle of them. It bumped into a red bag, then both packs flipped.

"Someone, page the office," said Mrs. Bowers, her voice shaking. "Whose backpack is that?"

Hayden glanced to the side to see if anyone would call him out. No way *he* was answering that.

Three girls ran to the phone on Mrs. Bowers's desk to page the office.

From deep in the pile of backpacks, Whiplash let out a growl.

"Get back," Mrs. Bowers yelled. Of course, Evan and Levi scooted closer. Hayden stood, ready to stop them if they grabbed his bag.

Please don't let anyone see Whiplash. Bringing a dragon to school was a *terrible* decision.

"Mrs. Bowers, you paged?" a voice asked over the intercom.

Whiplash let out another long growl.

"There's some kind of wild animal in my classroom," she shrieked, losing all composure. "Help!" She jumped onto her desk, sending a spray of papers to the floor. "Boys, *get back!*"

Hayden bounced on his toes with nervous energy. If he grabbed his bag and ran for it, everyone would know it was his. If he didn't, they'd find Whiplash, and his secret would be up.

His bag moved left, then over the red backpack. Several kids screamed, jumping onto their desks. Evan and Levi stumbled back, pulling each other out of the way as they fought to escape the growling backpack.

"We'll send someone right over," the voice on the intercom said over the chaos.

It was do-or-die time. Hayden opened his mouth and said the first thing that came to mind.

"There's a rat," he yelled. "It's huge!"

"Not a rat!" Mrs. Bowers screamed, then jumped from the desk to the filing cabinet and hugged the wall.

"It's under Seth's backpack!" Levi screamed.

Hayden's bag lay limp, but a blue bag scurried towards the wall.

Two large custodians burst into the room.

"Where's the animal?" the bigger man boomed. Mrs. Bowers, high on the filing cabinet, pointed to the corner.

"No!" Hayden cried before he could stop himself. He stepped into their path, not ready to lose Whiplash.

"Step aside, Hayden," Mrs. Bowers said with a shaky voice. "You're *not* saving rats!"

Heat climbed his ears at the snickers behind him. Sure, he'd saved all the mice from Mr. Turner's class last year, but that didn't mean she had to make it sound so *terrible*. Plus, Mr. Turner got his mice back and fed them all to the class snake before Hayden could develop a new rescue mission.

Both custodians moved past, clearing the discarded packs with gloved hands.

"Look at this, Doug," the smaller custodian said, pointing to a hole the size of a baseball in the wall. "I think it escaped through there."

Hayden's eyes grew. Whiplash had *escaped*.

The Great Hunt
6

He'd lost his dragon! Hayden shrunk into his chair as the rest of the room blurred around him.

Well, most of it. It was hard not to notice the janitors trying to talk Mrs. Bowers down from the filing cabinet. She swung her hands around like a dying bird, her voice raising to a whispered yell.

Any other day, the scene would be hilarious. Not today. The skin around his neck itched, like the frustration lying beneath the surface fought to escape. He ignored it and scratched his pencil into the desk.

He'd had the coolest creature in the whole world, and he'd been lame enough to think it'd stay in his backpack. Where would Whiplash go? The cafeteria?

Yuck! That place always stunk of oil and burnt food. Did dragons like the smell of burnt food? He sure didn't, but *he* wasn't a dragon. He'd check there first.

If he ever got out of this classroom.

And if losing the dragon wasn't bad enough, the new girl kept staring at him. Hayden glanced up, making eye contact for a split second—long enough to recognize the you-did-something-and-I'm-going-to-figure-it-out look. The same kind Makayla wore.

Makayla.

Just wait until she heard about this. She'd be all I-told-ya-so. A knot tightened in his chest. Maybe he should borrow the bathroom pass and search the halls to find Whiplash before she ever found out.

Seth leaned in and smirked. "Mrs. Bowers is going nutty."

"What?" Hayden turned in the direction he pointed. Mrs. Bowers climbed down from the filing cabinet but looked ready to leap if given a reason. "Oh, yeah."

"Don't worry, we'll trap the runaway rat," the bigger janitor said, walking to the door.

Trap?

Hayden threw his hand in the air, waving it for extra emphasis. He *needed* that bathroom pass.

"I'm done," Mrs. Bowers said the moment the janitors disappeared out the door. She collapsed in her chair and unwrapped a bar of the emergency chocolate she hid in her desk. "Recess is starting early."

Even better!

Hayden launched himself from his chair and squeezed through the doorway next to Seth, nearly pushing him over.

"Sorry, dude. Just heading for the hoops," Seth said, only slowing his speed walk a little. "You coming?" King of the hoops, he prided himself in getting to the court first and setting up teams.

"No, thanks," Hayden said, heading to the restroom. He ducked in and hid while the rest of his class rushed outside. School rules restricted kids from walking the halls during recess. But school rules also frowned on bringing animals to school, and he'd broken that one in a big way.

"Did you hear about the rat running around the school?" a voice asked.

Scrud. Someone was coming—and he knew something. Hayden hurried into a stall and locked the door. A shoe scuffed across the tile, and two boys entered the bathroom and hung out by the sink.

"A rat? No way."

"It totally attacked Mrs. Bowers," the first voice said over the sound of running water. A paper towel dispenser cranked three times before the tell-tale sound of the ripping paper. "And guess what? Benson said they could hear scratching in the walls of his class."

Scratching in the wall. Where?

Hayden flushed the toilet to not blow his cover, then opened the door. "Did you say a rat?"

Both boys glanced at him in the mirror. They looked familiar. Not fifth graders. Maybe younger brothers?

"Yeah," said a short and stocky kid with brown hair—the first speaker. The one that knew stuff.

Hayden stepped to the sink next to them and started the water. "Did you hear any scratching?" If he could get the kid to talk, maybe he'd lead him right to Whiplash.

"No. I'm not in Ms. Wilson's class."

Ms. Wilson, third grade. Bingo. He'd have to cross by the office to get there, but it'd be worth it. He turned off the water, wrung his hands, and wiped the rest of the water across his pants.

Don't look like you're sneaking.

Easier said than done. He tried to walk as normal as possible down the hall and past the office, but he couldn't help but walk-run when he reached the large glass windows. Somewhere behind there, Principal Whittle sat ready to bust recess-skippers, and he refused to be caught again.

Slowing, he rounded the bend that put him smack dab in the third-grade hall. Ms. Wilson's classroom waited at the end of the corridor, but there were no guarantees Whiplash was still there. He crept closer, turning his laser-sharp vision onto high alert. Boy, he'd give anything to have x-ray vision at that moment.

"Whiplash," he whispered, stepping closer. A shadow moved to his side. He flinched, then realized it was only the border of a bulletin board flapping in the breeze from the A/C.

Every muscle in his body buzzed.

He moved farther, his eyes scanning each and every ceiling tile and fiber of carpet.

Someone cleared a throat behind him.

He froze. *Caught.* Cringing, he spun slowly on his feet, fully expecting to see Mrs. Bowers, or worse, Principal Whittle, looming over him. His gaze followed the wall until it rested on . . . *Brooklyn?*

The new girl watched him with her arms folded. Then she pushed off the wall and walked closer to him. "It's Hayden, right?"

"Yes?"

The corner of her mouth twitched. "Not sure?"

The questions picked away at his patience. Whiplash was close by—doing who-knows-what—and he needed to keep moving while he was hot on his trail.

"Yes, I'm sure," he whispered, then he placed a finger to his lips. Now wasn't the time to have his cover blown. Recess wouldn't last forever, and there was a whole hall to search. He wandered farther into the third-grade wing, but she followed next to him.

Great, a tag-a-long.

"So," she started, her voice dropped to match his, "do you live close to the school?"

"Maybe." Why did she want to know?

An itch pricked behind his ear, and he scratched as he approached Ms. Wilson's classroom. He ducked next to the door and peeked through the side window. Empty.

"So, what kind of animal did you bring to school?"

Scrud. She knew. He needed to get her off his scent. "Animal, what animal?"

She slipped in front of him, completely blocking his view as she peered into the classroom. Her long hair tickled his arm, and he swatted at it. Swerving, she flipped her hair behind her shoulder. "Isn't that what you're looking for? Some lost animal?"

The way she studied him made him feel like a caged bird. She definitely knew something. He just wasn't sure what.

"I don't know what you're

talking about."

"Fine," she said with an eye roll. "Let's *pretend* you didn't bring an animal to school. Do rats typically hang out in the backpack closet?"

He shrugged. "It's a farm town. Mice and rats roam everywhere." That much rang true.

If the idea bothered her, she didn't let it show.

Fine, he'd make her squirm. "Sometimes, there are even *snakes.*" He drew out the 's' in snake to add extra flavor. "You aren't afraid of a snake, are you?"

She smirked. "A little reptile doesn't bother me."

So much for that idea.

"I can help," she said, turning to glance into Ms. Wilson's classroom again. "No one's in there. I'll be your lookout."

Warning bells went off in his head. A lookout sounded fantastic, but how could he trust her? Plus, if he agreed, she'd know he'd lied about bringing Whiplash. No way would he tell her the truth now.

But what *would* he tell her?

Hayden shoved his hands into his pockets and forced himself to think. His fingers wrapped around the coins he'd grabbed for the vending machine after school. The vending machine that waited right outside the third-grade doors.

Why hadn't he thought of that sooner?

"I think you watch too many kid spy movies," he said. "I was just getting a snack."

She narrowed her eyes at him. "A snack hidden in your pocket?"

Boy, this girl was aggravating. Hiding food in pockets was

so second-grade. He pulled out four quarters and jingled them in his hand.

"There's a vending machine just past the double doors," he said, pointing in the direction of the large glass doors with his chin. It was time for a new plan.

Fake a trip to the vending machine.
Lose the girl.
Find Whiplash.
Fake sick and go home.

The vending machine sat just outside in the corner of the building, darkened by the overextending roofline. She followed him, matching each of his steps. Annoying girl. Now he *had* to keep the charade up.

He pulled out the quarters and pushed one into the machine. It rattled as it cascaded down. Then he added another and scanned the options, not really sure what he wanted to buy.

A bag crinkled from behind the glass pane. Whoa. Had she noticed it, too? No—she seemed distracted.

He pushed the last quarter into the machine. As it rattled and crashed, something moved in the dark crevices. He rubbed his eyes and leaned closer.

Dark blue claws grasped the edges of a swaying bag of honey-roasted peanuts. Below, a long tail swung back and forth like a pendulum.

There was no doubt about it. He'd found Whiplash.

And the Secret's Out

7

Sharp claws sliced through the plastic package, spilling a waterfall of nuts pinging off metal machinery. No way Brooklyn would miss that. Hayden blocked the glass window with his body.

He needed to get Whiplash, and fast.

"Why are you acting so weird?" She asked behind him.

The dragon leap-frogged from snack to snack until he reached the bottom and started munching on nut pieces. Piles of wrappers and crumbs scattered around. He'd been busy.

She sidestepped one way to get a better view. Hayden quickly matched her movement.

What would happen if she knew? He could just show her his dragon. Maybe she'd help him.

Or maybe she'd tell.

She dodged the other way, and he followed, his brain spinning. Telling his sister worked out nicely. Besides, secrets were more fun when shared.

"Move," she said with a huff. "I know you're hiding something."

Fine. He'd show her—but only because there was no way he could rescue Whiplash without her knowing.

He shifted, giving her a full view of his dragon attacking a whole family of peanuts.

She gasped.

At least she didn't scream.

Then, she smooshed her forehead against the glass. "I knew it."

Wait—knew what?

"You stole my dragon," she said, pushing off the glass and shaking an annoyed look at him.

Hayden's insides bellyflopped. "Stole *your* dragon?"

Two third-graders skipped by with a giggle. Hayden jumped to shield their view. "Whiplash is *mine*," he whispered.

Brooklyn ignored him, giving all her attention to *his* dragon—who gnawed on another nut. The whole thing made him itch with frustration. Scratching the back of his ear didn't stop it; the itch only jumped from his ear to the back of his neck.

She tapped the glass. Whiplash looked up from munching but didn't give her more than a second glance before diving back into the snack.

Hayden clawed at his skin while a nagging idea clawed at his thoughts.

Why would she think his dragon was hers, unless . . .

"Did you move into the old Anderson place?" he asked. *Please be wrong. Please let her just be some crazy girl.*

Her eyebrow squished together. "The old what?"

"The Anderson place. The white brick house with the brown barn, all infested with mice." The last part might have been an

exaggeration.

She swiped at some dirt on the glass. "It's a good thing I have a cat then."

The room seemed to tip on its side and shake him a few times. Then it was true. She lived next door—the neighbor with a cat named Mr. Muffins.

He scratched the guilt itching around his collar. Yeah. He'd stolen her dragon.

No. He'd *rescued* Whiplash. The creepy sucking machine had caught on fire. Whatever she was going to do with the dragon, it clearly would have hurt.

And now he'd have to rescue him again.

Hayden sank to the cold concrete next to Brooklyn and inspected the opening. How on earth had Whiplash gotten in there?

"I gotcha, little buddy," he whispered. The dragon slithered to the pane and rubbed his head against the glass.

Good boy.

Hayden placed his palm on the glass next to his little friend and could almost feel his smooth scales. "I'll get you out of there."

Brooklyn's eyes narrowed on him.

"You know . . ." she said, her voice quiet but dripping with annoyance. He shoved his hand into the opening at the machine. A hard plastic plate separated him from his pet. "Mr. Muffins had a lot to say about the snooping neighbor boy."

Hayden lost his balance and smacked his face against the pane. "Your *cat* had lots to say?"

She shrugged, but the mischievous glint in her eyes hinted that she was messing with him.

Ugh. Girls!

"Did your cat tell you why I came to your house?" he asked. "I brought him home after your dumb cat tried to eat my pet."

His fingers slid along the edge of the plate until he came across a tiny opening. A keyhole, maybe? "Fetch me a stick. Maybe I can pry this open and get him out."

"Mr. Muffins doesn't eat dragons," she said, clearly not hearing his request—or not caring.

He'd have to use his fingernails. "Not Whiplash. The lizard," he said between clenched teeth. *Why wouldn't this thing pop open?*

She squinted at him. "Lizard? What lizard? Wait, you didn't find . . . a green lizard with an orange tongue?"

"Maybe."

Forget it! Prying the machine open with his fingernails would never work.

She stomped a heavy boot against the cement. "You did, didn't you? And you lost it!"

"*Your* stinking cat tried to eat it." Hayden waved his free hand. "Now get me a stick."

Brooklyn huffed but ran off and returned with a small twig in her hands.

"That's too wimpy," he huffed. Couldn't she have at least *tried* to find a decent stick?

The recess bell rang, and a stampede of kids started to line up near the classroom doors. Fine! He snatched the twig and jammed it into the opening. One push, then pop! The dumb thing broke.

"Mr. Jones, what are you doing?" asked a stern female voice. He yanked his arm out of the hole and jumped to attention in front of an extremely unhappy principal. Brooklyn pressed herself next to him, and together they blocked the glass window of the machine.

Principal Whittle stared at them down her pointy nose. "I had a friend who tried to sneak food out of a vending machine once," she said. "His arm got caught, and they had to use heavy-duty tools to get it out."

Hayden grimaced, picturing the large, angry janitor trying to get him out of the vending machine with a chainsaw. No, thank you.

Brooklyn nudged him with her elbow. *Was he supposed to respond to that?* His brain went completely blank.

"Hayden bought us a snack, but it got stuck," she said after a few uncomfortable seconds. She pressed a button on the machine, releasing a bag of Frooties Rooties, which splat against the metal bottom. "Look. All fixed."

Principal Whittle clicked her tongue then nodded. "You two need to line up."

He stood speechless until the principal rounded the corner of the building and disappeared. Brooklyn could have busted him and taken Whiplash for herself. But she hadn't.

"Thank you for saving my skin," he said.

"No problem." She grabbed the Frooties Rooties, then froze. "Umm . . . I think we have a problem."

She pointed through the glass. Crumbs and nuts were scattered throughout the floor of the machine, but *no dragon.*

Not possible.

He studied every hanging snack looking for claws or a tail. *No. No. No.*

He pounded against the glass and watched for any movement—still nothing.

"Let me try." She shoved the machine, rocking it the tiniest bit. They waited. Watching the back of the big machine was like watching a reflection on a blank television screen—boring and pointless.

"Where'd it go?" he asked and kicked the machine. Sparks of pain ignited in his toes.

"Look!" She pointed at the crumbs trailing out from behind the machine and down the sidewalk.

Whiplash had to be here, somewhere. He took a step back and scanned the walls. Besides a few fall leaves trapped in spider webs, they were bare.

Thousands of footsteps pounded against the concrete, coming right for them. Then, Levi turned the corner, and the entire class followed behind him.

"Dude, you better not try to cut," Levi hissed as he went.

The rest of the class passed in a blur. Hayden backed up until his shoulders grazed the jagged block wall. Evan passed, making kissy faces at him, then winked at Brooklyn.

Heat climbed Hayden's cheeks. He sidestepped away from Brooklyn and shoved his hands into his pockets.

"Get in line, you two," Principal Whittle said, bringing up the end.

"Where's Mrs. Bowers?" Seth asked.

"Gone home sick," she responded, flashing a fake smile. "Looks like you have me for the rest of the day."

Great. How would he ever find his dragon with the *principal* as a sub?

"I've got to find Whiplash," Hayden whispered, scanning the area one more time for any kind of hints.

Brooklyn nudged him and flashed a mischievous grin. "Not if I find him first."

Racing to Whiplash

8

Hayden scrambled into his seat across from Brooklyn. He acted as normal as possible, but his mind was freaking out. She wanted to find Whiplash first. No way he'd lose his pet now.

Well, except he already had.

His palm slammed against the desk with a satisfying thump.

"That's enough, Mr. Jones," Principal Whittle said. "Guys, take your seats. We've got a lot to cover and not a lot of time. Looks like Mrs. Bowers planned to jump into math, so we'll start there." She traveled around the room, rustling with a stack of papers.

He didn't dare take his eyes off Brooklyn. If he kept an eye on her, she couldn't sneak away to steal his pet.

She fidgeted in her seat, looking anywhere but at him. *What was she planning?*

"Do you have a class president or someone who helps with papers?" Principal Whittle asked.

Seth nudged him from the side. "Hey, isn't that your job?"

Hayden shushed him. What the principal didn't know couldn't hurt her.

Brooklyn raised a hand. "I think Hayden's the class president," she said, finally looking at him. A wicked glint flashed in her eyes.

"Alright, Mr. Jones," said Principal Whittle, sliding a stack of worksheets onto his desk. "I'd like you to pass these out to everyone."

"Thanks, man," Hayden whispered to Seth, who chuckled back. If his friend knew what was at stake, he wouldn't have been so happy about throwing him under the bus.

He swiped the papers and shoved his chair back. At least Brooklyn was just as trapped in the classroom as he was. He started counting sheets to match the number of kids and quickly passed stacks to each pod of desks.

"Yes, Brooklyn," Principal Whittle said.

Hayden counted two more pages with his eyes fixed on the devious new girl—the one having a secret conversation with the principal. *What were they saying?* It didn't matter how hard he strained to listen. He couldn't hear anything over the electric sharpener devouring a pencil.

Brooklyn stood, pushed in her chair, and walked to the front of the room. *Where did she think she was . . .*

She grabbed the one-and-only bathroom pass hanging by the whiteboard and sauntered out of the room, stopping only for a second to look back at him.

Oh no. She couldn't be.

Alarms in his brain screamed full alert. He dropped the rest of the papers onto Levi's desk. "Just take one and pass them down," he muttered. He had to get to the principal and get his own pass. Maneuvering around the pods, he tripped over the leg of a desk but caught himself before crashing into the ground.

A little tumble wouldn't stop him. If anything, it just made him look more desperate. Hayden jogged to the back desk, where Principal Whittle searched through Mrs. Bowers's lesson plans. Her finger slid across the teacher's curly writing, and she muttered under her voice.

"Can I help you?" the principal asked without looking up.

"I need to go to the restroom."

That got her attention. "You just got in from recess," she said with a heavy sigh. "I'm sorry, but you're going to have to wait for the pass."

Wait? There was no time to wait—not when Brooklyn had a head start.

Principal Whittle tapped a finger on a planner. "Found it." She snatched up a sticky note and stood to leave.

He had to act. It was now or never.

Hayden blocked her path.

"Please. It's an emergency."

Several heads turned their direction, and someone snickered.

He ignored them—there was too much on the line. Shifting from one foot to another, he pleaded with the best puppy dog eyes he could muster. The nervous shuffle probably looked like a potty dance, but all the better to make his case.

The principal watched him for the longest minute of his life. All the while, Brooklyn searched the halls free and clear. *She could have Whiplash right now.*

"I can't wait," he blurted out. More snickers. No doubt he'd regret that announcement later. "It's . . ." he gulped, debating how much he wanted this. No question about it. He needed to start searching. He lowered his voice to a whisper. "It's my stomach."

Principal Whittle pinched her fingers on the top of her nose and squeezed her eyes shut. "Go quick, Mr. Jones. And hurry back."

He bounced on his feet and zipped out of the room before she could change her mind. His mad dash would only add fuel to the boys' teasing later, but he didn't care. He had a dragon to save.

Rounding the corner of the hall, he looked both ways. White block walls decorated with bulletin boards and artwork formed a maze of options. Bits of paper and stray knit gloves littered the carpet, yet the halls sat empty.

Where had she gone? A silly thought bit at him. What if she actually needed to use the bathroom?

He sneaked closer to the girls' restroom, squeezed his eyes shut, and leaned into the doorway to listen. Muffled footsteps thumped against the tile, but he couldn't tell which way they were going.

Or whose they were.

This is silly. He should be searching for Whiplash, and instead, he's hanging out at the girls' bathroom.

Footsteps clicked on the tile near him.

"What are you doing?"

His eyes shot open at the sound of Brooklyn's voice coming from just inside the bathroom. "I'm lost?" he lied.

"You got lost?" she said, raising an eyebrow crossing her arms. "And ended up in the girls' bathroom? Maybe try walking around with your eyes open."

She thought she was so funny. "Did you find anything?" he asked. *Could his dragon be hidden in her pocket?* His eyes dropped to where her shirt hid the top of her jeans. No bulges or lumps.

"In the bathroom?" she asked and shook her head. "Nothing I want to tell *you* about."

What did that mean? He narrowed his gaze on her, then her empty hands. Had she found Whiplash or not?

"Rrrrrat!"

Frantic screams echoed down the hall. *Whiplash.* The cry sounded like it came from the teachers' lounge. Or maybe the office?

Hayden locked eyes on Brooklyn. She balled her fist and twisted her ear in the direction of the cries, then started sprinting down the hall.

He scrambled into a clumsy run. No way he'd let her get to his dragon first. He pushed himself into hyperdrive, channeling the best super-speed superpower, and flew right past her. *Ha! Served her right.*

Each step pounded on the tile matched the beat of his racing heart. The second the hallway opened up to the foyer, he skidded to a stop.

Glass walls surrounded the library on every end. There was no way they'd run past without the cranky librarian seeing. She busted every rule-breaking kid. And he'd know—she'd already caught him three times that month.

Brooklyn slowed to a jog but didn't stop. *Great. She'd* get away with breaking all the rules. New kids only got lectures and were sent on their way.

He peered through the glass—no sign of the librarian. All

clear. Speed walking as fast as his feet would go, he trailed after her.

The distance between them grew. He kicked it up a notch. How fast could he go before he was actually running?

He finally caught up to Brooklyn when they reached the hall leading into the teacher's lounge. The darkened hall taunted him. The whole area was completely off-limits. That was one rule he'd never considered breaking before. But he'd break it now if that meant he'd get Whiplash back.

"Move," she whispered, trying to get past him.

Oh, he'd move all right. Turning his ears on high alert—especially listening for teachers—he tiptoed down the hall and to the teacher's lounge. The words "teachers and staff only" hung on the door

What was a lounge anyhow? He imagined the room filled with big couches and televisions. Didn't lounging mean to lay around?

The handle turned without a sound, and the next thing Hayden knew, he was pushing the door open.

"I'm telling you," someone said from the front office that connected to the teacher's hall. "There's a rat in the break room."

Hayden froze.

"Did you actually *see* the rat?" a male voice asked.

"No, but something brushed against my foot and scurried behind the fridge." The desperate voice grew closer, along with clicking footsteps.

"Someone's coming," Hayden whispered. They needed to hide—now. He scanned the hall. A janitor's closet sat across the hall from the teacher's lounge. He shoved the door opened and darted in, pulling Brooklyn with him.

The door shut with a muffled thud, and everything went black. He bumped into shelves as he searched for a light switch, then kicked an empty bucket that rattled against the cement floor.

"Shh," she hissed. "You're going to get us caught."

He winced. She was right. He *hated* knowing that. And now he was stuck in a dark room—with a girl.

"Do you hear anything?" he asked. The only thing he could hear was his breath, which sounded a lot like Darth Vader running track. That is if characters from Star Wars actually ran track.

"Someone's talking," she whispered back.

Tuning in his super hearing powers—or lack thereof—he listened harder for any hints of sounds.

"We'll have . . . an exterminator . . ."

An exterminator?

Exterminate meant to kill. *They were going to kill his dragon!*

He heard them wrong. Killing animals at a school had to be a big no-no. *Mr. Scales ate mice at school all the time. That was killing.*

He leaned into the door and pressed his ear against the cold wood. *Please let me be wrong.*

The door opened, sending him flying. A large hand caught

69

his arm and pulled him upright.

Hayden fought himself free. His eyes focused on a large plaid shirt stretched across the biggest torso he'd ever seen. He scanned up, and up, and up . . . until he met the gaze of the large, cranky janitor.

Just my luck.

The janitor pulled his lips together in a thin line.

"What do we have here?"

Dragon Prints in Pink Frosting

9

R^{*un.*}

No, don't run! What was his brain thinking? Running was the *worst* idea. Hayden scratched at the back of his neck. Sweat ran down his collar bone, stinging his flesh.

The urge to run grew.

With Brooklyn next to him, perhaps they'd only get lectured. Maybe having the new girl with him would even lessen his sentence.

The janitor pinned them with a stern look. "I don't know what you two were doing," he said with a growl. "But it's not safe playing around in the supply closet." He shook his head. "Okay, look." His voice softened into something much less scary. "There are rats and frantic teachers, and it isn't even lunchtime. Today isn't the day for crazy antics."

He ran a hand across his enormous stomach. "Go back to class, and we'll just call this a warning."

A warning? Hayden didn't need to hear those fantastic words twice. Nodding, he started down the hall. The weight of those beady eyes following made him speed up a hair more.

Static buzzed through the janitor's walkie-talkie.

"Mrs. Whittle says to go ahead and put out the traps. I checked out our stock, and we're short. If we want to cover all the main areas and the cafeteria, we'll need more supplies. Did you find any in the supply closet? Over."

Traps? Exterminator. Hayden stopped, slammed his back against the wall, and waited for the janitor's response. Brooklyn paused next to him, leaning against his side.

"I'm looking in the closet, and it's a no-go," the large janitor replied. "I'll have to make a run for more traps. Over."

The heavy janitor closet door slammed, sending Hayden's pulse right into his throat. Rapid footsteps headed his way.

"Shh, follow me," he said, nudging Brooklyn's arm and started a new direction—into the foyer.

The janitor rushed past them toward the front door. "You two get back to class. No dillydallying," he said over his shoulder before pushing the large glass door open.

"Yes, sir," Hayden said with a nod. *Please let this work.* He slowed his steps and guided Brooklyn behind one of the large block columns. Then he dashed to another and ducked behind, hoping she'd understand and follow his lead.

"What are we doing?" she mouthed.

He peeked around and watched the janitor disappear into the parking lot. There was no way he'd come out of hiding until the large man drove off.

"Are you going to tell me why we're hiding in plain sight?" she hissed. "We're going to get caught, and I'm telling them it's all your fault."

Gee, thanks.

He should have just sent her back to class. Why hadn't he? Simple, if they set *traps*, he needed help finding his dragon.

"Whiplash is in danger," he said as he started sneaking back to the teacher's lounge.

"The traps . . ." she nodded, "but what does that have to do with us hiding behind the column?"

The itch from his neck jumped at his shoulder, and Hayden clawed at it. Everything about this day felt like a bad case of a rash. "It didn't. But I had to make sure that janitor-guy left."

"Well, he'll be back," Brooklyn said. "We better move."

His rubber sole shoe squealed as he spun on the tile. It was time to save Whiplash.

They sneaked to the hall leading to the teacher's lounge. Boy, what he'd give for an invisibility cloak. Then they could snoop around, and no one would know.

He hesitated at the door. *Teachers and Staff Only.*

And dragons.

Easing the door open, he peeked in. Nothing moved. No one talked. The room sat empty.

Hayden slipped through with Brooklyn right on his tail, then shut the door. The floor under his feet was slick and sticky at the same time. He turned and gaped at a *birthday cake explosion.*

"Wow. What happened?" she whispered.

Pink and white frosting mushed into the floor and smeared across the walls. A chunk of cake splatted against the ground, only inches from Hayden's worn-out running shoes. He looked up in disbelief. Cake clung to the ceiling above him, waiting to drop on unsuspecting teachers.

"I bet this was a killer food fight," he said, swiping frosting from the wall and licking it off his finger. *Yum. Vanilla.* The room smelled like frosting heaven, with maybe a hint of . . . hot chocolate?

"Look," said Brooklyn, hopping over a gooey glop of frosting and kneeling. "Lizard prints."

He snatched up more of the delectable frosting but paused mid-lick. Tiny prints zipped across the pink frosting and dotted the squares of tile.

"*Dragon* prints," he corrected.

They zig-zagged around chair legs and disappeared under a puddle of dark brown liquid. He sniffed the liquid. Yep. Hot chocolate. *Smells so good. I wonder if there is more.*

"We know he was here," said Brooklyn.

Might still be.

Hayden snatched an abandoned foam cup—the source of the sticky goodness. Tiny scratches lined the rim. Smart dragon, going after the best stuff.

He chucked it into the trash and pulled open a nearby drawer. "Whiplash," he whispered, finding nothing but boring towels and dishcloths.

Silverware crashed against wood where Brooklyn ripped a drawer open at the other end of the counter.

He rushed through drawers and cupboards, finding all the same things they had at home but without the cow print stuff Mom went all goo-goo over.

The last cupboard door slammed a bit too hard, and he

winced as the wham echoed.

"Did you find anything?" he asked.

"Just the snack bin." Brooklyn held up a bag of Flaming Hots corn chips. "Only fifty cents. Want some?"

He slumped. All she found was *chips?* There was much more on the line than the munchies.

"No. I don't *want* any." He ripped the fridge open and scanned the stacks of Tupperware without actually looking for anything. Anger and frustration fogged his vision. Whiplash was lost somewhere in the school. They were so close but still had nothing to go off of, and it was all *his* fault.

He slammed the refrigerator door.

"Shh. Did you hear that?" Brooklyn asked, a powdery orange finger to her mouth.

Freezing, he listened for scratches or dragon squawks.

Just a few feet away, the door cracked.

Hayden gulped back a scream.

Static sounded, and the door stopped. "Can someone please check the bathrooms?" Principal Whittle's voice blasted through a walkie-talkie. "I have two missing kids, boy and girl. Start with the boy's bathroom. I think that one might be sick. Over."

Hayden's body went into statue mode—every muscle freezing in place. *This was it.* He'd be caught in the very forbidden, very destroyed teacher's lounge, covered with frosting. Forget trying to prove to Mom he was responsible. He'd be grounded for a month.

Maybe a year.

"I'm on it," the voice said from the other side of the door.

Steps faded away. Hayden listened for any other noise—

nothing. *Get back to class!*

Time was up. But if he left, Whiplash could get caught. Or worse.

A hand pushed him from behind. "Just go." Brooklyn reached past him for the door. "We'll find him during lunch."

Yes. During lunch.

With night ninja moves, Hayden crept out of the break room and started down the hall. The bathrooms sat to the right.

He dashed left. No sense in running into a trap. Sure, it would take longer, but he'd cut through the lunchroom and make it around before getting caught. Brooklyn matched his run-walk pace as they flew past the copy room and slowed at the cafeteria door.

"We'll sneak through here," he whispered, gripping the long handle of the cafeteria. "Our room is just on the other side. Ready to run for it?"

Before she could answer, he pulled the heavy door open. The room smelled like burnt grease—just like every other day. But, without a room full of kids to dissipate it, the aroma almost made him gag.

He plugged his nose and bolted, cutting between round lunch tables. At the other end, he flung the doors open with a little too much force. *Oops.* But another few steps, and he'd be safe back in class.

As he entered the classroom, he released a long breath and tried to calm all his jitters. Classmates worked in groups on some project involving balloons and long strips of masking tape.

Pop!

Seth struggled to juggle balloons with one hand and tape

with the other. Catching sight of Hayden, he started frantically waving, scattering balloons all over the ground.

Whoa. They'd made it.

Hayden turned to give Brooklyn a conspiratorial high five . . . but she was *gone*.

Flamin' Hots and Dragon Tails
10

Where was Brooklyn? Had he left her behind? Lost her in the lunchroom?

Hayden leaned out of the classroom and scanned the hall but saw nothing.

"Welcome back, Mr. Jones," Principal Whittle said from right behind him. "Your team has missed you."

Oops.

Levi grabbed him around the neck in a completely unexpected side hug. "Yeah, your team missed you," he said in an annoying high-pitched voice. Then he laughed and released his hold, getting back to his group.

Whatever that was.

"Yeah, I . . ." There really wasn't anything else to say.

She sighed and gestured to Seth. "Go join your pod team. You have some makeup work, but you might as well enjoy the STEM activity."

"I've got the boy," she said into the walkie-talkie. "Has anyone checked the girls' bathroom? Long dark hair, black clothes. Over."

Hayden wanted to hover near the principal and wait for the answer, but she urged him on with a stern look.

Now he'd lost Whiplash *and* Brooklyn. He sunk into his seat.

"Hey, dude. Get over here. I need your help," Seth said, squishing a balloon between his torso and elbow with one arm while simultaneously ripping a long piece of tape. The tape pulled free from the roll, curled, and attached itself to his arm. He tried to shake it free, but it clung. "We only have a few minutes to build the tallest balloon tower, and I've already popped two balloons."

The balloon in his arm popped. He rolled his eyes and huffed. "Make that three."

Hayden pulled the roll from Seth's hand and tore off a long piece of sticky white tape. "Give me that balloon. I've got this."

Adding another to the tower only made it sag more. *This will never work.* He picked up the top of the tower and gave the entire thing a gentle shake, hoping to strengthen it somehow. From over the green balloon, he saw Brooklyn sneak into the classroom, the Flaming Hots still in hand.

Her chip bag jostled.

He dropped the balloons.

"Dude," Seth said. "It's dying. Pick it back up."

"Oh, yeah." Absentmindedly, Hayden lifted the balloons. His eyes narrowed in on the chip bag.

Brooklyn slipped the bag of chips behind her back and snuck to her backpack. When she shifted to stash the snack, a dark scaley tail slipped between her fingers.

She had Whiplash!

He squeezed the balloon too tight.

Pop!

"Pop any more balloons," Evan yelled, "and you two will have to build your tower out of tape."

Seth held up a new balloon and grinned. "I grabbed spares."

"Sweet," Hayden responded as he scratched his neck, only giving his friend half his attention.

"What's that on your neck?" asked Seth.

Hayden paused mid-scratch. "What's what?" Purple goop stained his fingers and smeared over his nails. *Frosting?* No. The stuff stuck between his fingers looked more like a fleck of jelly.

Oh, *that's* what the hug was all about. Levi and his pranks! Whatever guys. He stamped down the temptation to glare and just wiped the goop onto his jeans.

All the while, Brooklyn and Principal Whittle had *another* secret conversation in the back of the room.

"I'll be back," he said, kicking the balloons that hovered by his feet. Seth moaned something under his breath at him, but Hayden was on too much of a mission to hear it.

Principal Whittle scribbled something on a pad of paper, ripped the sheet off, and handed it to Brooklyn. "Take your backpack with you, sweetheart. I hope you feel better."

No! The principal had given her a one-way ticket out of school with *his* dragon. Brooklyn nabbed her backpack from the cubby, escaping through the door. Right before the door closed, her sick façade broke into a sly smile.

"Looks like your girlfriend is sick," Levi said, nudging Hayden with his elbow.

"She's not my girlfriend," he spat back. He shouldn't have even trusted her to be a friend.

Defeated, he plunged back into his seat and smacked his forehead on the cold surface. Maybe he could pretend he was super nauseous and corner the thieving girl in the nurse's office.

"One minute on the clock. Then we'll see how everyone's done," Principal Whittle announced.

"Hayden. Dude. Help!" Seth yelled.

He blinked up at Seth.

Any other day and he'd jump all over this project, but today he felt as deflated as the balloon guts spattered all over the floor.

"Come on!" his friend yelled. He ripped off another long piece of tape and held it out to Hayden.

"Thirty seconds."

Hayden grabbed the tape.

Seth threw a balloon. "Put it somewhere on top. I don't care where."

"Ten. Nine. Eight." The principal's countdown only added more stress and chaos to the room.

Hayden taped down the balloon.

"Time," she called through cupped hands. "And, it's lunchtime. We're going to have to pause this experiment and take measurements when we get back."

Lunchtime. Free time.

He eyed the clock. Brooklyn had a two-minute head start. He might be able to catch her. And if anyone asked him what he was doing, he could say he was checking up on her for Principal Whittle. Perfect.

Lunch box in hand, he found his place in line.

"You playing ball at lunch?" Seth asked, taking his spot behind Hayden.

Several students crowded in on the principal, freaking out over cheaters messing with their balloon tower. The whole scene was slowing the lunch train down.

Seth nudged Hayden's arm. "You've been acting weird today."

"What?" he asked, trying to shake off his friend's comment. "Basketball? I don't know. Maybe. I'm not feeling too good. I think I'm going to the nurse's office."

If we ever get to leave. Hurry it up.

The principal kept nodding her head like a toy bobblehead and repeating that all the towers would be okay. Too bad no one seemed to listen. He glanced up at the clock. A whole other minute had gone by.

"Dude. Are you going to the nurse because Brooklyn's there?" Seth asked a little too loudly. "You guys keep disappearing together today."

"Told you she's his girlfriend," Evan called from somewhere behind them. Hayden rolled his eyes and flexed his hands. *Ha. We weren't even friends.* Not after she stole his dragon.

Tick-tock, this was dragging on.

"You can go ahead," Principal Whittle called to the line.

You don't have to ask me twice. Hayden practically mowed over the kids in front of him to get out the door. When the group turned left to go into the cafeteria, he escaped to the right, swerving around the other fifth-grade classes to get through.

All the way to the front office, he mentally replayed the karate moves he'd use to get Whiplash back. Boy, he'd show that thieving girl who was boss.

He peeked inside the office—the secretary's desk sat vacant. In fact, no one seemed to be around at all.

Perfect. That made it even easier to sneak behind the counter and down the hall. He poked his head into the nurse's office.

Empty.

Where in the world was Brooklyn? Dread filled his stomach like a pile of rocks. She was gone. Whiplash was gone.

Hayden backed out of the nurse's office.

"Mr. Jones, what are you doing back here?" Principal Whittle asked as she headed to her office. At least her voice wasn't all angry.

"Just coming to check on Brooklyn," he said, replaying his practiced words.

"That's great that you two made friends, but she's gone home," she said. Then she narrowed her eyes at him. "You wouldn't know anything about loose rats today, would you?"

The hallway closed in tight. Principal Whittle seemed to grow taller and tower over him. He pulled at the hem of his shirt behind his back.

"Rats?" he said slowly, a lump forming in his throat. "No." *Not rats, but dragons.* A half-truth was still a part-truth, so technically, he wasn't lying.

She watched him longer until he almost gave a full confession under the weight of her stare. But the static buzz on the walkie-talkie kept his words from escaping.

"Caught a rat. Over," a voice said.

"About time," the principal muttered, charging down the hall.

Someone caught a rat! Wow. At least he knew it wasn't Whiplash stuck in a mousetrap. Hayden remembered the machine he saved the egg from—in Brooklyn's barn. If it wasn't one trap, his buddy was definitely caught in another. He needed to get Whiplash back.

The Return of Mr. Muffins
11

The rest of Hayden's school day lasted an eternity. Thank heavens for early release, though getting out early only meant having his sister rub in her I-told-you-so's sooner.

Makayla's mouth dropped open like a dying fish. "Let me get this straight. The new neighbor is in your class, and she stole Whiplash?"

"Yes. Now stop talking about it," he shushed her, pulling the lock off his bike. Kids huddled around them, gathering scooters and bicycles. No one seemed to pay them any attention, but he didn't want to chance someone hearing.

They walked their bikes along the wide sidewalk that circled the parking lot. The whole time, Hayden struggled over what to do next. Would Brooklyn hurt Whiplash? Was he okay now?

"We have to get him back," he said as they approached the beginning of the fast zone.

"Didn't you steal the egg from her?" Makayla whispered.

He cringed, stopping right in the middle of the sidewalk.

Kids flew past, shooting dirty looks. *Oops.*

"I don't know," he whispered, moving his bike to the side. "But Whiplash is mine. We spent all night hanging out. He knows me. I can't just let him go without trying."

She pulled at the streamers hanging from her handlebars and sighed. "How do you even plan to get him back."

He'd spent the rest of school scheming and came up with exactly zero plans. But she didn't need to know that. "First, we should go home and check in with Mom," he said. "After that, we'll sneak over to the old Anderson place and see what we can find."

"You mean *spy?*" Makayla clapped her hands and bounced on her toes.

If he'd known spying would get her on board, he'd have mentioned that to begin with. "Yeah, lots of spying."

She jumped onto her bike, a huge smile blasting on her face, and rocketed down the sidewalk. Hayden followed, winding around the walkers. Leaning forward, he tore a path across the rough asphalt and raced the familiar trail home.

The old Anderson barn came into view. Today, the large wooden doors were barred closed, exactly how it sat for the year—like yesterday never happened.

Makayla swerved, making a big figure-eight right in front of the neighbor's barn. He shook his head—*so much for being discrete*—and turned into the gravel driveway to their house.

A flash of orange fur streaked past him, nearly colliding with his front tire before leaping into the bushes. Hayden slammed on his breaks, but his tire caught on a loose rock, sending him flying over the handlebars. Sparks of pain shot from the shoulder that smashed against the sharp gravel.

He rolled to his back and blinked back tears as a shadow hovered over him.

"Are you dead?" Makayla asked, her face all puckered up like a raisin.

"Yes," he whispered back. *And death hurt.*

Pebbles stuck to his mangled flesh. He brushed them off and hissed when he grazed the large gash on his arm.

Mr. Muffins scowled down at him from the fence rail.

"Stupid cat," Hayden said. He picked up a rock and chucked it across the lawn. The aim was bad, missing on purpose, but he'd didn't want to hurt the annoying feline. Just scare him.

The cat smiled back.

Hayden rubbed his eyes. Cats don't smile. Obviously, he'd hit his head much harder than he'd thought. He scrambled to his feet.

"You're all bloody," said Makayla with a wince. The color drained from her face. Even her freckles looked ghostly.

Dark red blood stained his hand, and he swiped at the thick liquid racing down his arm. *Forget investigating the barn.*

"Are you okay?" Mom yelled from the door.

Great, he had an audience. Even better. He forced himself not to cry.

"Hurry in," she called. "I'll clean you up."

Hayden sat in the kitchen watching Mom shuffle through the first aid kit looking for bandages big enough to cover his scrapes. Blood ran from his shoulder, pooling at his elbow and threatening to drip on his pants. It stung like fire, but he'd have major awesome battle scars.

Makayla left the room, claiming she had homework. Yeah, right. He knew the truth. She just couldn't handle the sight of blood.

"Here." Mom's soft whisper gave a two-second warning before a warm washcloth swiped across his stained hand. Hayden leaned against the hardwood chair and squeezed his eyes shut. She held the cloth in place for a minute, and the burn slowly eased.

Sometimes having a mom wasn't so bad after all.

"Principal Whittle called today," she said, the moment his pain finally disappeared.

His eyes flew open. "Yes?"

Mom slid the wrapper off the bandage like she hadn't just thrown a stink bomb into his thoughts.

"She says someone might have brought a rat to your class today." She paused, her eyes locking on his. "Was it you?"

For once, he didn't have to lie. "A rat?" he said with a shake of his head.

Mom went back to work on his arm. "I told Principal Whittle you would *never* bring an animal to school. I hope I wasn't lying."

Panic bubbled in his stomach. *Never bring an animal.* That was different than asking about a rat.

"I didn't bring a rat to school," he said with a little too much anger in his voice. "I swear."

One of her eyebrows raised, and her lips pinched together. She rested her face in her hand, biting her lip and watching him. He smiled at her, but it faltered. She had to believe him. He *wasn't* lying. He hadn't even touched a rat.

"There's something you have to learn to have a happy life—" Mom started.

"Truth and trust." He rolled his eyes. "I got it." The truth only ever got him busted. There was no way he'd fall for that one.

Makayla bounded into the kitchen. "Hayden. Can you . . . um . . . help me with my math?" she asked, nodding her head toward the hallway.

Mom looked from Makayla to him, then back again.

"Makayla, sweetheart," she started, her voice very sweet

and pleasant, not the lecturing voice he'd just endured. "Do you know anything about Hayden bringing a rat to school today?"

A lump of saliva formed in Hayden's throat as he waited for his sister's answer. Makayla knotted her hands together and shook her head no.

"Well, good." Mom stood and started gathering up the first aid kit. "After the big mouse rescue in Mr. Turner's classroom . . . well, I just had to check." She ruffled his hair on her way to the counter.

He stood to leave but stopped. She'd totally fixed him up and dropped the rat thing.

"Thanks." He pointed at his bandaged-up arm.

She turned back to him with a huge smile. "Call me Dr. Mom. But be careful."

Grabbing his uninjured arm, Makayla pulled him towards the living room.

"And Hayden, you need to clean behind your ears," Mom hollered to him. "Looks like you tried to eat a jelly sandwich with your neck."

He rubbed a hand over the back of his neck. Bits of purple jelly speckled across his palm. He put it to his nose for the sniff test and gagged. *Oof! Not jelly!* Wiping it on his pants left a dark stain on his pant leg—no biggie. He rubbed his neck again to get the rest of the wannabe jelly off his neck.

Weird and gross. Maybe he landed on something in the road? Road guts? *That could be cool.*

Makayla practically drug him to his room. "What's the deal?" he asked. "You've never asked me for help with math in your life."

She held a finger to her lips, closing the door behind him.

"What?" he mouthed.

Screeeech.

What in the world? He turned just in time to see. Muffins pressed against the window, one paw scratching the glass.

"I think he wants in," Makayla said.

Hayden stared at the fat tabby, then pounded on the glass to scare the cat away. Instead, Mr. Muffins nudged the window with his head.

"Scat, cat!" he said through the glass. Holding up his bandaged arm, he added, "You've done enough today."

Meow.

"Do you think he's stuck?" asked Makayla, petting the glass where the fluffy orange hair pressed.

Hayden pressed his nose against the pane to get a better

look. "I don't think so."

Mr. Muffins thumped his head against the window. *Meow.*

Hayden jumped back. "Is that . . . *normal?*"

The cat shook his head, then puffed his chest and stood at attention. *Cats don't understand humans like that, do they?*

"Get the ninja sword from under my bed," Hayden whispered, frowning at the cat.

"Ninja sword?" Makayla's voice rose and twisted into a question mark.

"If I'm going to open this window," he started with his hand out, ready for the sword. "I want to be prepared."

She reached under the bed while Hayden waited, wrapped up in an intense stare-off with Mr. Muffins—and the cat was winning. The feline's tail waved an innocent swaying rhythm, but Hayden wouldn't be fooled. That little devil nearly killed him thirty minutes ago.

"Got it," Makayla whispered, handing him his favorite weapon.

Hayden took the plastic blade, the weight giving him a sense of comfort. Sure, it wasn't heavy enough to hurt the beast, but if Mr. Muffins attacked, at least he wouldn't be empty-handed.

Sword ready, he eased the window open.

Mr. Muffins leaped right past Hayden and his trusty sword. Then the stinking cat jumped up on the bed, circled around, and plopped to the comforter.

"I thought you'd never let me in," the cat said in a deep voice.

Did He Just Speak?
12

Makayla strangled Hayden's arm with incredible super strength. He pried her off but shifted to shield her from the talking cat.

A talking cat? Impossible.

"Wha . . .who are you?" he asked, stumbling on his words. His brain felt like scrambled eggs with melted cheese.

The cat yawned. "You already know who I am. What you really want to know is *how* I am talking."

The animal had a point. But instead of explaining, the mangy feline just continued to flick its catty tail and wait for him to beg for an answer.

Hayden waved an impatient hand. "Well?"

"It's a long story," Mr. Muffins said with a bored yawn. "Let's just say it has to do with Dr. Slade."

"Who's Dr. Slade?" Makayla asked, stepping around Hayden. "Wait. Is that Brooklyn's dad? Is he . . . like a wizard or something?"

"Yes and no." Mr. Muffins said with an annoyed flick of his

tail. "And that really isn't any of your business. Is it? Just like that egg wasn't any of your business before you stole it from the incubation machine."

Hayden's heart dropped to his toes then leaped to his throat. So, it wasn't a death machine after all? "Where did Dr. Slade find a dragon egg?"

"Find it?" The cat chuckled, or more like cackled. "You don't *find* dragon eggs. Clearly, you don't know anything about biology."

"Do you mean Dr. Slade *made* the dragon egg?" Makayla asked.

"No, Dr. Slade didn't make the dragon," the cat said with a smirk. "Brooklyn did."

Now *that* was unexpected. Hayden slumped to the bed next to the cat, his legs turning to jelly.

"I told you that dragon belonged to someone else," his sister whined, pacing back and forth and wringing her hands.

"How could Brooklyn make a dragon?" he asked. "That's not even possible."

"Once again, the expert," said Mr. Muffins with another roll of the eyes. "Moments ago, talking cats were impossible, too. The simple answer is . . . science."

Somehow, that one word was supposed to magically answer all his questions? Science didn't create mythical creatures. Not in Hayden's world. The only experiment he'd mastered was mixing baking soda with vinegar to watch it bubble. It was awesome but didn't exactly conjure up wings and a tail.

Wait. If she could make a dragon, what else could she make?

"Don't get any crazy ideas," Mr. Muffins said as if he could read his mind. "The Slades aren't in the business of making magical pets."

"Are they in the habit of reading people's minds?" Hayden bit out.

The tabby only licked his chops and smiled at him. Infuriating animal. Just like his owner.

The cat laughed. "No. I can't read your mind. But I don't have to. Everything is written on those freckles on your face."

Makayla giggled, pointing at Hayden's nose. "Maybe it's like dot-to-dots."

"Very funny," he growled back. "Your face is just as speckled as mine."

She pressed a hand to her face, covering only half the rust-colored spots sprinkling over her cheeks and nose.

Mr. Muffins stood, stretching his back and then each leg. "Don't get your freckles in a knot. I'm only here because that dragon you stole is going crazy."

That brought back the strength to Hayden's legs. He stood tall, hovering over the cat. "What did you do to Whiplash?"

"Whiplash?" Mr. Muffins huffed. "Why do all the other animals get the good names, and I'm named after food?" The cat sauntered across the bed. "And we didn't do anything to that temperamental lizard with wings. He's ping-ponging around Brooklyn's room, destroying everything."

Hayden suppressed a smile. Brooklyn wanted him to rescue her from the dragon. Maybe if he proved he could control it, she'd let him keep it.

"And don't even get me started on the fireballs." Mr. Muffins leaped from the bed to the windowsill and gestured with a curled paw. We need to go."

Did he say fireballs? Sweet. Hayden met Makayla's eyes and smiled wickedly. This he had to see. And fireballs could only mean one thing—s'mores.

"We need marshmallows," he said, snapping his fingers and moving to the door. "Oh, and some of Dad's hidden Halloween chocolate." Dad always bought chocolate during the first week of October and hid it in his sock drawer—like clean socks would stop him.

"This isn't a family campout." Mr. Muffins slipped out of the glass onto the ledge. "We've got to go!"

Makayla hovered at the window. "Do you think he wants us to climb down the apple tree? That's like a thousand-foot jump to the branches."

Forget that. It was one thing to *climb* the tree. It's a totally different thing to Superman it out the window and hope to not die. *I vote to 'not die.'*

But the cat was leading him to his dragon.

"We'll meet you downstairs," he said to Mr. Muffins, then closed the window.

The cat leaped from the windowsill to the tree and scaled the limbs. Hayden watched until the cat turned back and hissed.

"Right. We should probably . . ." He pointed to the door.

Makayla bounced ahead of him. "I can't believe I get to see a real mad science lab. Do you think Brooklyn can make me something?" She squealed. "What if she has a unicorn hidden in her bedroom? Do you think she'd let me ride it?"

"Shh," he said with a yank of her arm. "Mom might hear you."

"So?" She pulled her arm free from his grip. "Like Mom

is going to believe our neighbor has a *real* unicorn in her room. No one believes me when I say they are real."

Hayden searched the hall for any signs of Mom.

"I'm not sure Brooklyn wants everyone to know about her lab," he whispered. "I think it's a secret."

"Oh," she said, then motioned zipping her lips shut.

He followed her down the stairs but paused at the landing. "Do we have any marshmallows?"

Makayla shook her hand at him and crossed her arms. "I thought you were joking about that."

Hayden turned to her in disbelief. She clearly missed the bigger picture. "And miss my opportunity to eat a dragon-roasted s'more? I kind of don't think so. Plus, Whiplash loves chocolate. It might be the way to calm him down."

Her lips stretched into a big, toothy smile. "I'll grab the marshmallows and graham crackers. You sneak the chocolate."

Yes!

Hayden high-fived the air and raced back up the stairs. He pushed his parent's door open and dropped to his knees at the sound of Mom talking. Thankfully, her voice became muffled, like she'd gone into the bathroom.

He crawled into the room just enough to assess the situation. If Mom caught him, he'd just say he was playing a game with Makayla.

Except for Mom's voice, the room stood empty. Dad's dresser sat next to the bed. If he scrambled over, he'd have the mattress to shield him. *Go!*

He rustled to the bed. The bathroom door opened.

". . . a *rat*," Mom said.

Hayden twisted around and peeked over the bed. A light cut past the door, but there was no sign of Mom—*time to hurry.*

"Of course, I told Principal Whittle that he wouldn't. But after the whole mouse fiasco, she didn't exactly sound convinced."

Slowly, he raised to the top drawer and pulled. The stupid thing squeaked!

The bathroom door flung open. "Just a second, honey."

Crumbs! He dropped to the floor.

Mom's shadow dimmed the room. He closed his eyes and scratched his neck. Footsteps padded across the carpet toward him. The itch spread like fire from his toes to the end of his rust-colored hair. He fisted his hands to keep from scratching. Mom came closer. This was it. He was doomed.

Something scratched against the glass of the window.

Meow.

"Oh, for the love!" She gasped. "Oh, nothing. Just a cat in the window. I think I'm losing my mind, but I swear it just winked at me."

Mom's voice faded away. She must have gone back into the bathroom. But was there really a cat at the window?

He peeked over the bed. Sure enough, Mr. Muffins stood just outside. The cat locked eyes on him and snarled.

Busted.

Hayden scratched at his chest. The tingling and tickling raced to his back.

Just grab the candy and run.

Slowly, he slid the drawer just a crack and shoved his hand to search out Dad's secret stash. He found two chocolate bars and went back for more. *Maybe sharing chocolate with the cat will keep him from clawing my eyes out.*

"I hope I wasn't lying to the principal," Mom said through the door. "I just never know anymore. I want to believe him."

Ouch. Her words stung. She didn't believe him?

"I just hope I haven't made a huge mistake thinking he was finally ready."

Ready? Ready for what?

Thump.

He blinked back to reality. Mr. Muffins banged his head against the window again.

The bathroom door whipped open.

Hayden dropped to the floor as Mom stepped out, the phone at her side.

Great. He was stuck.

Everything Itches

13

Hayden lay on the floor, staring at Mom's feet from under the bed. They were so close. He could reach out and grab her.

And be grounded for life for freaking her out.

She moaned, dropping something on the bed, then marched to the window. "Go away, creepy cat."

Whack.

Mom's hand slapping the windowpane nearly made Hayden's heart explode. *Get out of this room—now!* He watched her feet, which were now all the way across the room—the perfect distance.

Meow.

Rising to his hands and knees, he peeked over the bed. Her back was to him. *Good.* Sweat burned a line down the back of his neck.

Go!

No need to tell him twice. He scrambled on stealth mode across the floor. The moment he jetted out the bedroom door, Mr. Muffins let out a high-pitched hiss.

Mom screamed. The bathroom door slammed.

Chocolate-handed, Hayden booked it down the stairs and out the front door, nearly tripping on Makayla.

"Here." He crammed the stolen chocolate into the grocery bag that dangled from her wrist.

Her eyes widened to the size of pancakes. She bit her lip and giggled. "Did you get caught?"

"By the stalker cat," he said between puffy breaths. "Yes."

It suddenly felt like a thousand ants tangoed across his back. He squirmed and danced to ease the tickle, but it didn't help. Maybe ants really *were* dancing on his back.

To make things worse, his sister just kept laughing like he was crazy. Couldn't she see he was suffering? He scowled at her and rubbed his back on the rough wood column on their porch.

Ahh. Relief.

She stopped laughing and frowned. "Are you okay?"

"No thanks to you."

A blur of orange leaped from the tree onto the grass.

"Get lost?" Mr. Muffins asked, scaling the porch railing.

Makayla lifted the grocery bag slightly. "Just getting supplies." She winced and looked to Hayden for help.

Okay, on the surface, his s'more idea seemed bad. But if the chocolate calmed Whiplash and helped him win his dragon back, it'd be worth it.

"We don't have all day," Mr. Muffins said, jabbing a paw in his direction. "My crazy cat trick in your mom's window is only good for one go. If I keep repeating that, people will notice."

Makayla scrambled down the stairs, but Hayden scratched a moment longer, leaning to the left and getting that last spot.

Yeah. Right there.

"You coming?" she shouted to him.

Just one more scratch. The tingling traveled up his spine and to his neck. Ugh! He pushed off the post and chased after them.

Mr. Muffins scaled the fence that ran between the two houses— the same fence the cat smirked at him from when Hayden crashed.

And that whole time, the annoying cat had understood what he'd said.

"Have you always been a cat?" Hayden asked, running behind his sister.

Mr. Muffins hesitated mid-step and scowled at him. "Yes. I've *always* been a cat."

Hayden ran his hand through his hair, something felt . . . different. *Lumps?* He gulped and traced a finger over each individual lump on his head. *Were those horns?*

"Dr. Slade can't turn me into an animal or something?" he asked, counting the bumps—five.

Mr. Muffins licked his chops. "If he does, I'm voting for a fat country mouse."

"Can he?" Hayden persisted.

"No. Or if he could, he wouldn't. But now I'm craving mouse," the cat said with an evil grin, then started back across the fence.

"Very funny." Hayden dropped his hand. Thick goop clung to his fingers. Too thick or purple to be blood. Clearly, he wasn't getting the jelly goop from pranks or landing on it in the road. *What was going on?* He rubbed the junk on his jeans. Might as well—he had a whole goop family smeared across his leg at this point.

Makayla stopped ahead, staring at the barn. He hurried to

meet up with her and the mangy cat, then slammed on his breaks.

Whoa. New boards crisscrossed over the large door. A heavy padlock met in the middle, shutting off the dark and mysterious room he'd broken into yesterday.

Mr. Muffins meandered between his feet, tickling his ankles. "Dr. Slade didn't exactly take well to having neighbors snooping in his lab."

"His *lab?*" asked Makayla, twisting the bag in her hand. "It's in there?"

"Yes, and he isn't going to be too excited seeing you here again." The cat started ahead of them. "I'll try to buy you time. Go inside the house and find Brooklyn. Top of the stairs, first door on the left." Then he wedged through a small hole at the base of the barn door and disappeared.

"Okay, so the front door," Makayla whispered, tiptoeing around the side of the barn. Her steps crunched on the gravel driveway leading up to the barn and house.

Hayden tried to make his steps as light as possible. Maybe Dr. Slade wouldn't turn him into a country mouse, but maybe he *would*. He didn't want to find out.

They inched around the edge of the barn.

Gravel crunched behind him, and Hayden choked on a breath.

"Ah, it's you again," a deep voice growled behind him.

So much for the cat saving the day.

The tingle of nerves charged down the side of his neck. He glanced over his shoulder.

Dr. Slade stared down at him, looking even more menacing behind a dark welding shield. The big purple lumps he'd seen yesterday danced along the flesh peeking out under the shield.

Hayden's own skin seemed to wiggle. He slapped a hand to his neck and backed away from the large man.

"What do you want now?" Dr. Slade asked. "More snooping?"

"I'm just . . . just here for Brooklyn," Hayden squeaked. Ugh. If he ever didn't want to sound like a scared mouse, it was now.

He peeked around for some sisterly support but found himself alone.

Where was she? Inside?

The front door waited cracked for him.

"You're looking for Brooklyn?"

Hayden shifted to look back at Dr. Slade. No, not at him, but at the big purple eyeball size lump jiggling on his collar bone. The doc placed a hand over the sore. "I'm glad she's making friends." He tilted the welding shield up slightly, and Hayden could feel the man size him up. "I guess you'll do."

Do for what? Hayden stepped back. If the good doctor thought he could run an experiment on him, well, he was mistaken.

The shield lowered back over Dr. Slade's face, and he waved at the door. Hayden didn't need any other invitation. He turned and bolted to the house.

Makayla opened the door wider as he approached. "Way to help me out there," he whispered as he passed her.

She wrapped the bag around her hand so

tight, the marshmallows were probably smashed-mallows. "He gave me the heebie-jeebies, so I ran." She wrinkled her nose and leaned into him. "What's wrong with your neck?"

Her gaze made his skin twitch. "Nothing," he said, covering it with a hand. Warm stickiness dampened his palm, and he instantly thought of the weird dancing lump on Dr. Slade's neck.

His brain was playing tricks on him. Obviously, people's skin didn't turn purple or ooze out goop. *Or grow horns.* Still, he wasn't going to let her get a better look. Shielding his neck from her view, he passed his sister and crept up the stairs.

Some people were allergic to cats. Maybe hugging genetically altered—*talking*—cats made him extra itchy. And turn purple. *Yeah right.*

Get Whiplash. Go home. Make this all go away.

Mr. Muffins snaked past Hayden's legs, disappearing into a cracked door. The first one at the top. Brooklyn's room.

"Hello?" he asked, gently knocking on the door.

Nothing happened.

"Whiplash? Brooklyn?"

Still, nothing.

He pushed against the door and did a double-take. This wasn't a bedroom, but an office. A desk sat against one wall with a computer next to stacks of some boring books on science and math. Even crazier, a table rested against the wall, covered with test tubes, a microscope, and weird-looking knickknacks.

So, not an office. A lab.

A large whiteboard full of scribbles hung on the wall near the door. In bold purple ink, he read the words "Hayden—Friend or Enemy?"

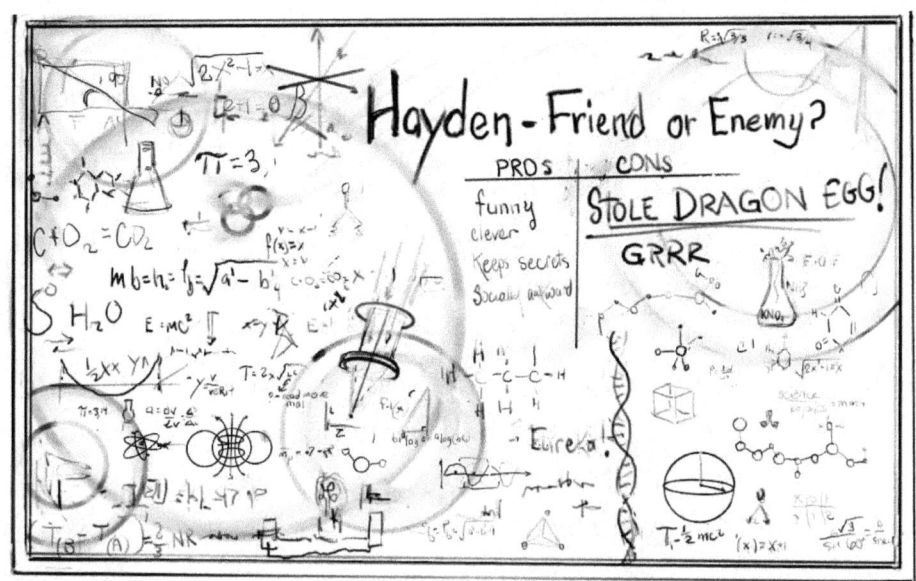

Friend or enemy? Ha!

He stepped into the room and waited for Makayla to follow before closing the door behind him. Soft beeps and a low buzz definitely fueled his imagination, but it was his name printed on the whiteboard that caught his complete attention. Underneath, a list of pros and cons teased him. He needed to know what they said.

Pros:

Funny.

Clever.

Keeps secrets.

Socially awkward.

Wait? Socially awkward was a pro?

His gaze switched to the cons, and he winced. In all caps, the words *STOLE DRAGON EGG—GRR!* were written and underlined. Twice.

Yeah, that probably wasn't the best way to make friends.

He picked up the eraser. Maybe he could fix the list, or at

least erase the *grr!* He swiped at the letters, finding a secret joy in seeing them disappear beneath the rag. Then the air shifted, and the closet door flew open.

Hayden recoiled. Makayla squeaked. Brooklyn stood there with an eyebrow cocked and her arms crossed.

"Looks like I need to add 'touches things without permission' to my list." She rolled her eyes and held her hand out for the rag.

He didn't budge, not sure what to say or do. Where was Whiplash? And Mr. Muffins?

Brooklyn waved her hand again. "The eraser. Before you decide to mess up my equations, too."

He slid the rag into her hand but didn't release his grip. "I'm here for Whiplash."

She frowned at him and tipped her head to the side.

Girls were infuriating.

"My dragon," he added.

"Oh," she said, pulling the eraser from his grasp. "I think you mean *my* dragon."

Test Tubes and Sticky Goo
14

"What do you mean, *your* dragon?" asked Hayden, biting down his sudden urge to yell at her. "Your cat told me you needed me to rescue you." He scanned the ground, looking for any movement. Nothing. "What did you do to him?"

The door behind her remained open, reminding him of her weird entrance. Why had she waited in there like some sort of creepy closet monster ready to pounce? Wait a second . . . Whiplash must have been in the closet! He sidestepped, but she mirrored him. He tried the other direction, but she blocked him.

Heaven help him. If Brooklyn didn't move, he'd charge right through her. An itch crawled from his ear to his shoulder, and he couldn't help but rub at it.

The more Hayden scratched, the bigger her eyes grew. "How long have you had that rash?"

"He's been itching all afternoon," Makayla said from behind him. "And he's starting to look like a jelly-jam sandwich."

He did *not* look like a jelly-jam sandwich. Right? Hayden

dropped his hand, secretly wiping the purple slime-snot on his pants. Brooklyn stepped back, like he was contagious. *Girls.*

"Whiplash? Buddy. Are you okay?" he called to the closet, ignoring the head-to-toe itch that tormented him. Raising himself to tiptoes, he tried to look over her, but she shifted to block his view.

Were those burnt holes in her shirt? Ha! He would rather be a jelly-jam sandwich than burnt toast.

"You should probably stop scratching, or it's going to spread," she said.

"I'm just allergic to your stinking cat," he said. *Or turning into a goopy monster like your dad.* Hayden ignored that nagging thought and gestured at her shoulder. "Have a little problem with some fireballs?"

She slapped her hand over the hole. "Nope." The upturn of her nose and the way she blocked his view screamed that she was lying.

He smiled, stepping closer, and sniffed. "Then why do you smell like burnt beef jerky?"

"Oh, knock it off," Makayla said, stomping up to him. "My brother isn't always so cranky. He just really wants his pet back."

"What she said—" Hayden nudged his sister with his elbow. "Just give me Whiplash . . ." *and tell me what's up with your dad's face,* "and I'll get out of here."

He folded his arms to make a point, and his hip jammed against the large table covered in lab stuff, rattling the glassware.

"Careful," Brooklyn said, steadying the table. "Tip over the wrong vial, and you'll be instantly frozen."

"A Hayden-sicle. Not nearly as good as a mouse, but I could

get into that," Mr. Muffin added, sneaking out of the closet. "Oh, and you owe me gummy bears and chocolate milk."

Brooklyn rolled her eyes and pulled the opinionated furball into her arms. Hayden peeked to the closet again, getting a better view now that Mr. Muffins had left the door almost completely open. He did a double-take. Her closet had a *bed* in it?

"You sleep in the closet?" he asked, his mind trying to process each piece of the puzzle being thrown at him.

"Oh, I want to put my bed in the closet. Do you think it would fit?" Makayla asked, rushing to the closet to get a better look. "Eek! And your dresser is in here, too! It's like a room inside a room. And I love your pictures on the wall. Is that a picture of you at your last school?"

Hayden tuned out Makayla, and her non-stop chattering and focused on the vials and tubes on the table. "Did you say 'instantly frozen'?" he asked.

Mr. Muffins jumped from Brooklyn's arms onto the table next to Hayden, expertly missing a big jar of a neon blue liquid. "Yes, she said 'instantly frozen.' And before you say that's impossible, just remember you're talking to a cat about a dragon."

Good point.

Hayden examined the table. Bottles and jars neatly labeled with purple ink lined one side of the table. Gadgets and machines cluttered the other. Every bit of it looked mysterious and exciting. And he basically wanted to touch everything.

But even more, he wanted his dragon. She had created one. She could make another. He'd never be able to do that, not in a million years.

"Where's Whiplash?" His words came out in more of a

growl, and he regretted it the moment Brooklyn scowled at him. "I'm sorry," he added, relaxing his shoulders and rubbing the sore below his ear. "It's been a long day. Please let me see that he's okay."

"That cranky lizard with wings is just fine," Mr. Muffins barked.

Brooklyn shot a glare in his direction. "No thanks to you." She swept her hand and gestured at the room. "But my lab definitely isn't."

For the first time since entering, he noticed the papers and books scattered around the floor—like a mini dust devil blew through. Just like the teacher's lounge. Red streaks oozed down the wall, meeting paper confetti sprinkled all over the floor. The bookshelves looked just as haggard—the books spilling over the edges.

"That dragon went insane and bounced around my room like a rocket on Independence Day. Then, it just crashed."

Crashed? That sounded painful.

"Where?" Hayden pushed past Brooklyn and into her tiny closet-bedroom.

Makayla grinned up at them from where she sat on Brooklyn's purple comforter. "Shh," she said with a finger over her lips. "Whiplash is sleeping." A shoebox rested on her knees. Inside, Whiplash snored on a small fuzzy pillow.

"And that was *after* he tried killing me with a couple well-placed fireballs." Brooklyn flipped her long black hair, uncovering her other shoulder and several tiny burn holes in the black fabric. "It's probably a good thing he's only a baby."

"Or that your hair didn't catch fire," Makayla added.

Hayden bit back a laugh at the mental image of Brooklyn running around in circles with her hair flowing behind her in flames. He'd definitely enjoy dumping a bucket of water on her head to get them out. Especially after the chip bag thing.

Mr. Muffins joined Makayla on the bed. "The evil monster looks so innocent now."

Hayden tried to imagine Whiplash pinging around the room. Sure, he had done some damage at the school, but *how?* Every time Hayden had seen him, the dragon seemed mellow and happy.

"What's your plan with Whiplash?" Makayla asked, running a finger down one of the tiny dragon wings. The dragon fluttered his wing and squirmed before letting out a loud snore.

"My plan?" A wicked smile crossed Brooklyn's face as she turned to Hayden. Whatever she was thinking, it wouldn't be good. "I want to analyze him."

Analyze?

He knew it. She was going to hurt Whiplash. He clenched his jaw and tried to devise a plan. Maybe he could snatch Whiplash and make a run for it. Except then, he wouldn't know why he was covered in exploding purple-goop-bumps.

"Why do you need to analyze it?" Makayla asked.

"Science." Brooklyn scooped up the box from her and studied Whiplash from the side. "I want to see what it's capable of. Record everything."

"Nope." Mr. Muffins said, shaking his head like a never-ending bobblehead. "Do I need to remind you? Fireballs!"

"Yes, but this time we have a different target," Brooklyn said, her smile growing until her teeth showed.

Teeth? Ha! More like fangs. She planned to use *him* as target practice if Whiplash woke up in a fiery mood. Forget that. He'd be taking his dragon home now.

He reached for the shoebox imprisoning his little friend, but she blocked his move and carried Whiplash out of the mini bedroom. Hayden followed. He'd wait until she was distracted, grab the box, and run. Makayla could follow his lead.

Brooklyn slid the box onto her desk next to the closed laptop, and a rag stained deep red.

Makayla turned ghostly pale and gagged. "Is that . . . blood? Do scientists use blood?" She slid down the wall into a puddle of girl on the floor and rolled herself into a ball. "Don't use my blood."

"What?" Brooklyn picked up the rag and flung it into a laundry basket. "Blood? I'm a scientist, not a witch. It's black cherry punch." She ran a finger on the table. "And it's going to leave a sticky mess."

She muttered something about an obnoxious dragon tornado and straightened the books on the shelf. Hayden eyed the box.

This was his chance—grab the dragon and go. He'd figure the rest out later. That's what the Internet was for, wasn't it?

Makayla laid all balled up on the floor, not noticing his attempts to make eye contact. Forget it. He'd have to leave her and hope she forgave him later.

"Here, I'll hold Whiplash while you scrub the desk." He raised the box slightly, hoping he looked innocent.

"Right," Mr. Muffins said from the bookshelf. "And I just stalk birds because I enjoy bird watching."

How had he forgotten the clever cat would be watching him?

Brooklyn didn't notice—too deep in thought while she haphazardly scrubbed the surface. Probably thinking about using him for target practice.

"How'd the drink spill anyhow," Hayden asked, setting Whiplash's bed back onto the desk. "Weren't you worried about ruining your laptop?" If he had a laptop, he'd protect it with his life. Then again, he'd never have a laptop. Not when his mom's favorite word was "no."

"Oh, that's not where I left my drink." Brooklyn huffed in frustration and glared at the sleeping dragon. "I had it over on the table. This is just what was left over from his explosion. Well, and the stuff on the ceiling. But at least it stopped raining juice."

Talk about a whirlwind of crazy. All because of a baby dragon.

"Whoa." Makayla unraveled herself and stared up at the ceiling. "Are those dents up there from Whiplash, too? I didn't know he could fly!"

"He flew?" asked Hayden, his eyeballs popping out of their sockets.

"I definitely wouldn't call it flying. One sip of that punch, and he was a dragon ping-pong," Brooklyn said, hovering over Whiplash with a magnifying glass. "It *looks* like a dragon."

Of all the stupidest things . . . "Of course, it looks like a dragon. That's because it *is* a dragon."

She set the magnifying glass aside and pulled out a purple notebook, completely ignoring him while she scribbled notes on the page.

"I know it's a dragon. But this one actually *looks* like one." She started sketching Whiplash, then added his wings. "Not like the last couple."

"The last couple?" Makayla asked, jumping off the floor.

Wait! She'd made more? And more importantly—if there were more, could he keep this one?

Dragon Pox
15

"We have to wake him," said Brooklyn, and she slammed the pencil into her notebook. "It's the only way to observe him properly."

"Whoa there," Mr. Muffins said, leaping from the bookshelf onto the floor. He scrambled through the closet door and under Brooklyn's bed. "I'll just watch from here."

"Scaredy-cat," she muttered under her breath. "You're ready, right?" she asked Hayden. Her face had turned more ghostly, if that were even possible, and she fidgeted with her pen.

Strange.

Hayden pushed Whiplash's box along the table closer to her. She flinched backward.

So, she was afraid of the dragon, too. Good, now he could get answers. "First, tell me about the other dragons. And, what's going on with your dad's face?"

She blanched. "I have no idea what you're talking about." Her reply was all sing-songy—just like his sister when she tried to pull a fast one. He scratched at the small rash behind his ear and then followed the tingling down this neck. The itch would never leave him alone.

But man, it felt good to scratch.

Brooklyn made a face and stepped further away from him. "Stop scratching. You're just making it worse."

Makayla pointed a finger near his skin, hovering so close he almost felt it, and scrunched up her nose like she'd just smelt a rotten egg bomb. "Yeah, your neck looks all *lumpy.*"

He waved sticky fingers at Brooklyn, then inched Whiplash closer. "Tell me what's going on, or I'm touching you. Then I'll wake the dragon and aim him right at you."

Brooklyn backed up and moaned. "Fine. I'll tell you." She dropped her hands, shook her head, and sighed super dramatically. "But only because you clearly can't keep from scratching."

He wished she'd just spit out whatever it was. All the waiting only made him itch more.

"You've got the pox," said Brooklyn.

Makayla giggled and wiggled her finger next to his throat. So annoying. He smacked her hand away.

"Not possible," he replied. "I already had the chickenpox, and everyone knows you only get it once."

Right? Or was that smallpox you only got once? Why did so many illnesses have the word "pox" in them?

"Just show him the book," Mr. Muffins's muffled voice called from the closet.

"Always bossing me around," Brooklyn grumbled, rolling her eyes. She walked the few steps to the bookshelf, then stopped. "You can't tell anyone what I'm about to show you."

Was she serious? Everything about today fit in the "keep it on the down-low" category. He pointed to the whiteboard. "Pro: Keeps secrets. Remember?"

"Yes, well, those were just first observations," she said with a wave of the hand. "Theories that haven't been tested yet."

Theories? The weirdness factor of this day shot to a new level—a feat considering everything else that had happened. Brooklyn was just plain nutty, but in a cool, mad-scientist meets secret agent kind of way.

"Plus, what about her?" She pointed at Makayla.

His stomach belly-flopped. Of course, he'd forgotten about his sister and her inability to keep secrets. Makayla pleaded to him with her eyes—all puppy-doglike and sad. No way could he fall for that.

But she didn't tell Mom about Whiplash.

In fact, so many times today, she could have told on him, but she didn't. A smile pulled at his lips, and he nodded to his sister. "Makayla's good. You can trust her."

His sister rushed at him and dive-bomb hugged him. "Thank you," she squealed, tightening the hug into a wrestling death grip. Then, she released him with a hiss. "He's not contagious, is he?" She looked at her possibly diseased hands with disgust.

"Not contagious," Brooklyn said and pulled out a book that screamed: *I'm full of ancient mysteries* and *open me at your own risk*.

A spark of excitement jolted through him. Oh yes, he'd risk it.

"I mean it," she said, hugging the book in her arms. "The only people that have seen this book are me, Dad, and Mr. Muffins—if you count him as a person."

"Heard that," Mr. Muffins said.

Hayden waved off the cranky feline. "You can trust us. Plus, we already know about Whiplash and Mr. Muffins."

Brooklyn opened the book and laid it on the desk. Makayla leaned over Hayden for a better look, and he moved to let her in.

"This is my grandpa's science journal, so don't get any crazy ideas about taking it."

He balled his fists. "I don't *steal* things."

From the closet, Mr. Muffins cackled. Brooklyn raised an eyebrow.

"Fine, I don't *usually* steal things."

"Whatever," she said and flipped through the book. "The point is this journal doesn't leave this room." Ink sketches stretched across several stained pages as they flashed by, but Hayden couldn't make out what the images were. He really wanted to shout "slow down" so he could soak in all the awesomeness. That would have to wait for another time. Once he didn't itch so badly.

She stopped on a page and pointed. The bolded words *Dragon Pox* dominated the top of the page. Three sketches followed—one of a dragon, another of a man covered in pox, and then a sketch of a pair of human hands covered in . . . *scales?* Penciled words and confusing math symbols were scribbled between the sketches.

"What's dragon pox?" Makayla asked before he could.

He ran a finger just above the pox-covered image, remembering the nasty sores poking out from Dr. Slade's collar. Under the drawing, he caught the words "Don't get wet—it will speed the process up" underlined twice, followed by "extremely itchy."

No kidding.

Brooklyn looked up at him. "It all starts with an infected glitchy dragon. Not all experiments go well." Her white cheeks turned raspberry red, and she nodded to the box where Whiplash stirred. "Actually, that's my first glitch-less dragon."

Glitch-less?

Makayla squinted and shook her head. "What does *that* mean?"

Brooklyn sighed. "The first couple of eggs didn't hatch. Then Dad and I got lucky, and one hatched, only it didn't have wings." She growled and pushed the mysterious book-of-awesomeness aside. "Do you know what a wingless dragon looks like?" She grabbed her own journal and opened it and slammed her finger on a sketch of a lizard.

Not any lizard—*his* lizard. Okay, well, not really *his* lizard, but the one he nearly caught. And he would have if it hadn't been for Mr. Muffins.

Wait . . . Did that mean the cat was trying to *save* him from turning into the jelly-jam man?

Brooklyn nudged the notebook to the side. "No one takes you seriously when you tell them you're making a dragon, and it hatches without wings. Especially when *all* my experiments end up . . . wrong."

Makayla turned the sketch of the wingless dragon so she could see it better. "What happened?"

"The first dragon glitched. Dad touched it first." Brooklyn said, grabbing her notebook and slamming it shut. "Now he has the pox. That's basically it."

Okay, that explanation isn't helpful at all.

The closet door creaked open, and Mr. Muffins's face peaked out. "Is it safe?"

Brooklyn nodded.

From the corner of his eye, Hayden watched Whiplashed wiggle in the box. He should say something. But if he did, Brooklyn might shelve her grandfather's journal and any answers to his current situation.

And maybe Whiplash was just stirring in his sleep.

Mr. Muffins bounced onto the desk, circled the page once, then pawed the image of the pox. "Does extremely itchy ring a bell?"

Both girls stared at Hayden's neck, making it burn more. *Why does everything itch more when you try not to think about it?* It was like a family of spiders crawled down his neck and across his arms. He couldn't take it anymore and started scratching like he'd never scratched before.

Brooklyn grabbed his hand. "Don't scratch. It spreads." The stern expression on her face said she meant business.

"You think about spiders crawling across your skin and try not scratching them," he said and clawed harder.

"He's not going to give them to me, is he?" Makayla asked, looking at him like he was some kind of mutant.

Brooklyn tapped to some scribble in her book. "No. Only a glitched dragon spread the pox."

"Specifically, the one your brother fought me for yesterday," Mr. Muffins grumbled and flicked an annoyed tail. "I tried to save you. You're welcome." He licked his chops and grinned. "I'll take gummy bears as payment."

"Gummy bears?" Hayden asked with a snort.

"Well, you took country mouse off the menu, so I'll take what I can get." Mr. Muffins rubbed a nonchalant paw across the page. Talk about haphazard. If he kept it up, he might smudge the words off the entire page. "I like to bite their heads off."

I'm sure you do.

"So, let's say I have dragon pox—" Hayden started.

"You do," Brooklyn said.

He glared at her. Just because she says he had dragon pox didn't mean he wanted to admit it out loud. ". . . how do I get rid of them?"

Brooklyn shoved Mr. Muffins off the book and turned the page, exposing a new full page of scribbles and stains. "I haven't figured it out yet. It's bad enough that I keep messing the science up, but now I've infected Dad, and I can't seem to stop the change."

"*Change?* What did you do to me?" He rubbed his shoulder against his jaw to help stop the constant tickle. Somehow knowing he had the pox made everything much more tickly and annoying.

"Listen, hotshot," Mr. Muffins said, barring his teeth. "You should know better than picking up stray animals in trees. Consider this a natural consequence. You could have gotten rabies or something worse."

"If dragon pox turns my face into a slimy volcano," Hayden

said. "I kind of think that's worse than rabies."

"Much worse." Makayla made a face that resembled how he felt when Mom added mushrooms to a meal. "Everyone at school is going to think my brother is a goop monster."

If Mom even let him go to school like that. Even worse, Mom might take him to the doctor, where they perform tests.

"We've got to find a cure." He pulled the book away from Brooklyn and flipped the page back and forth. The smudged mark had left it completely illegible. Panic sparked. "Where are all the words?" he shouted.

Cluck! Squawk!

Mr. Muffins jumped to attention, his ears twisting. Whiplash staggered across the wood table with a face fire engine red.

"No!" Brooklyn shouted before ducking. A single fireball shot across the room. Hayden pushed his sister and dodged out of the way. Mr. Muffins hissed and sprang into the air. The fireball met the tip of the orange fur tail. Instantly, the fine hairs burst into flames like a kitty-torch.

Makayla sprung to her feet and ran to the closet. "I'll get the marshmallows!"

Smoke and flames trailed Mr. Muffins in a giant loop-de-loop of smoke and flames. "Yooooowl!" He rounded the room one last time, then jetted right out the window.

Brooklyn screamed and ran to the window as Hayden snagged his dragon. He sprinted next to her and held Whiplash at the ready. If more flames spit from the dragon's mouth, it'd be better if they flew outside.

Below, Mr. Muffins hung from the side bucket, half-drowned, his orange fur plastered to his body. He struggled to climb out

of the water between coughs and sputters.

"So much for the s'mores," Makayla said, leaning over the ledge. "Or do you think the cat will object if we try again?"

"S'mores?" Brooklyn asked, looking between Hayden and his sister as they turned away from the window.

Makayla held up a bag of Unicorn Marshmallows and shrugged. "You know. Because of the fire." Brooklyn scowled at the bag, then back at his sister. "What? It was his idea."

Whiplash coughed a few tiny sparks. "Aim that thing away from me," Brooklyn said with a shaky voice.

Heavy footsteps sounded next to the door, followed by three rhythmic knocks.

Crumbs! Dr. Slade.

"Hurry. Hide the dragon," Brooklyn whispered, throwing her purple journal over the big leather book on her desk.

What about hiding myself?

Makayla threw him the shoebox. He set Whiplash inside and slammed on the lid—just as the door opened.

Lumps and Scales

16

"**B**rooklyn, have you seen grandpa's jour—" Dr. Slade's words slammed to a halt the moment Hayden made eye contact with the man. With quick movements, Dr. Slade spread the papers in his hands out in front of his face, like a weird scientific fan masking everything from his eyes to his collar. That didn't stop Hayden from getting an eyeful of the green scales with patches of skin between them covering his cheeks and neck.

Scales! Dr. Slade was the incredible lizard man.

Hayden couldn't help staring. His mouth was doing that open guppy thing, but he couldn't help it. Would he turn into an incredible lizard man, too?

"Nope!" Brooklyn shouted. She cleared her throat. "I mean, I don't have any journals in my room."

Dr. Slade studied Hayden, leaving him feeling completely exposed. Did the lizard man see his bumps? Or had he seen Whiplash? Hayden slowly slid the box behind him, wishing he could hide the pox as easily.

Now all they needed was for the drenched cat to join the fun and unleash an angry list of frustrations on the room.

"You still have friends over. I'll just . . ." Dr. Slade fumbled with the doorknob, clearly not sure if he wanted to come in or run. It was weird for an adult to act so nervous, but if the doctor ran off, that was a-okay with Hayden.

The box began to twitch in his hand, and the skin of his neck burned like fire. It was like everything wanted to gang up on him. He fought the urge to scratch his skin or, better yet, the desire to rip those papers from Dr. Slade's face to see just how bad the scales were.

From this angle, Hayden had a petty good view of the man's disgusting neck. He swallowed a gag.

Look away.

Why didn't his eyes obey his thoughts?

Gross. Was that pus? Yep. Lots of purple pus ran down the sides of Dr. Slade's neck and pooled at his collar. *Was it pus first and scales later? And why doesn't he just wash that nastiness away?*

Duh! According to the super-secret—and apparently stolen—journal of awesomeness, getting the pox wet was a big no-no.

Hayden pictured his face covered with the same sores. He just wouldn't get them wet. Sure—no problem. Who needed a shower anyhow?

Brooklyn walked to her dad and whispered something in his ear.

"Okay, but only for a little bit." He scanned the room. "And you need to clean up your la—room. A good scientist never leaves their *bedroom* in this much disarray. Are you sure your grandpa's book isn't in here? I'm looking for," he shot a glance at Hayden and Makayla before continuing, "a certain entry of no importance whatsoever."

Hayden wanted to roll his eyes and laugh. Grownups were just as awkward and silly as kids—hoping no one read between the lines of their clumsy codes.

Brooklyn shook her head "no," but the fingers crossed behind her back screamed, "yes."

Somehow the lie-not-lie did the trick, and Dr. Slade backed out of the room, the paper fan blocking the lower part of his face until the door closed.

Hayden sagged.

"I don't think I've ever been so scared in my life," Makayla whispered. She stared at the door like she expected it to swing back open any moment.

Brooklyn grabbed her grandpa's journal and hugged it tight. "Tell me about it. I've been hiding this book for two days. As Dad changes, he's started making more . . . mistakes."

"What do you mean *changes?*" Hayden asked, touching the skin beneath this chin. It felt normal, didn't it? Was he changing, too? *Changing into what?*

Brooklyn dragged him into her closet-room. The room was so tiny—there was really nowhere to go but on the bed. He flopped onto the purple comforter next to Makayla, not loving that Brooklyn wasn't explaining herself. She obviously *knew* something. He set Whiplash next to him, then put all his energy into his best spill-the-beans look.

She shut the door and bit her lip. "He's turning into a dragon. If we don't cure him soon, it'll be too late." Her eyes connected with Hayden's with a look that sent warning bells off. "And you're next."

Makayla gasped and scooted away from him, like he'd already grown wings or something. He ran a finger over the bumps under his hair. Well, he had grown *horns*.

He gulped. "I'm turning into a dragon?" Of all the times he'd dreamed of getting superpowers, he never thought he'd actually have the opportunity to turn into a magical beast. But now, the idea gave him a stomachache. "Can we stop it?"

Brooklyn climbed onto the bed next to him, flinching when she realized how close she was to Whiplash. She scooted a half-inch away and flipped the journal back to the page with Dragon Pox scribbled across the top. Then she turned another page.

Hayden studied the smeared mess.

"All I can make out is the word 'tears.'" She pointed at faint scribbling.

Makayla leaned over Hayden to get a better view. *At least she wasn't worried about me infecting her.* "Tears?" she asked. "But I thought water was bad. Why would you want to cry?"

Oh, there were lots of reasons to cry. He'd cry now if it weren't so embarrassing.

"I don't know," said Brooklyn with a shrug. "It doesn't make any sense. There's more written here, but I can't see any of it." She pulled the book off her legs and onto the bedspread. "It's like grandpa was playing a trick on me. Like he knew I'd infect Dad and didn't want me to figure this out, so he wiped all the words away."

Whiplash crawled free from Hayden's hands and scampered to the book. His long tail whipped around, and he started chasing it in clumsy circles over the page.

Brooklyn finally relaxed and laughed. "He acts like a dog."

"Yeah," Hayden said with a chuckle and scratched under Whiplash's chin. The dragon rolled over and batted at his fingers. "A puppy that pretends to be a rat at school and throws fireballs at cats. This guy is all mixed up."

"No. He's perfect," she said with a velvety soft voice. "He's the first experiment I've done on my own without glitching it. I want to show Dad and prove that the kids at my last school were wrong. That I have what it takes in the lab." She groaned. "But I can't until I fix the *last* mistake I made."

Hayden understood. Sheesh, the need to prove to his parents that he could raise a pet was the only reason he was in this mess. The only reason he talked his sister into spying on the neighbor.

Spying.

A thought bubbled inside him. It was crazy, but everything about today was crazy, so maybe that's what they needed.

"Have you guys ever seen those spy movies with kid detectives?"

Makayla sat up and nodded. Of course, she had. His sister lived for those movies. Brooklyn, on the other hand, looked confused.

"Remember how they get information written on pages when they can't read the writing?" He directed the question at Makayla, hoping that she'd understand what he was thinking.

His sister thought for a second. Then her face lit up. "Oh, yes! Yes! They look at the next pages for indents from the pen pressing against the pad of paper." Her smile faltered. "But how can we do that?"

Brooklyn sucked in air and giggled. Girls always giggled at things when it made no sense.

"You're a genius," she said. "Grab Whiplash. I want to turn the page."

A genius! Mental fist bump.

Makayla scooped up Whiplash, and Brooklyn grabbed the book. She examined the illegible page, turning it back and forth. For being a genius, Hayden had no idea why she alternated pages like that. Wouldn't she just need the reverse page? That's what they did in all the spy movies *he* watched.

Then she did something insane—she slowly *ripped* the page *out* of the book. Forget the happy fluttery heartbeat—now he was suffering a heart attack. They were in for it.

Scratch that. *Brooklyn* was in for it.

If this boat sank, she'd go down with it alone. He had nothing to do with ripping pages out of the extra stolen, ultra-secret family books. Panic skipped up his back and tickled at his neck. Without thinking, he touched the spot.

"Don't. Scratch." Makayla slapped his hand.

"I'm not scratching." *Yet.* He ran a finger along the back of his ear, up and down the bumps that had grown much taller than before. "What are you thinking? Aren't you afraid of getting busted?"

She slammed the journal shut. "I'm going to run an experiment on this. Then we'll have our answers. It's brilliant. Then, Dad will forgive me, because . . ." She held the ripped page up triumphantly. "Answers!"

And at *that* moment, the door opened.

Fuzzy Note Decoder

17

The page ripped from the super-secret, super-awesome science journal looped as it dropped to the ground. Brooklyn's eyes grew to the size of baseballs, and Hayden was pretty sure he looked the same.

The door bounced open.

But no one was there.

"It's either me or that flame-throwing beast. There's no way we're both sleeping in this room tonight." Hayden's gaze dropped from the doorknob. A mangled version of Mr. Muffins glowered up at them. "Don't worry about getting me a towel or anything. I'll take care of myself."

Mr. Muffins climbed onto the bed and rolled his wet body over Brooklyn's pillowcase.

"Thanks for that lovely gift," she said with a gag.

The cat ignored her, rubbing his fur back to a semi fluffy state, then stretched. "Did I hear someone yell for marshmallows while my tail was burning? Yeah, I think I'm going to just lay here on your pillow for a bit longer."

Brooklyn shook her head and snatched the paper off the floor. Apparently, she didn't want to deal with the ever-cranky Mr. Muffins either.

"Okay, let's do some science."

About time. Hayden clapped his hands and jumped off the bed. "Let's do this thing." The words flew out of his mouth before his brain could tell him to dial it down. Luckily, Brooklyn only laughed at his excitement and led them back into her lab.

"Oh no, you don't," Mr. Muffins called after them. "You aren't leaving me in here with that . . . *thing.*"

Oops.

Hayden rushed back into the closet and peeled Whiplash off Mr. Muffins's head, where he had started to bite Mr. Muffins's ear. *Five points to the tiny dude for taking on the lion.*

"Can you grab the gummy bears off my dresser?" Brooklyn called from the other room. "We can snack on them as a celebration when this works."

Mr. Muffins spun onto his stomach and prepped himself to pounce. "Those are mine. I earned them."

Angry feline eyes stalked Hayden as he nipped the bag from the dresser and slipped past. He tossed the treat bag onto the desk—a few of the colorful treats escaping onto the wood—and hurried back to the action.

Makayla had snagged the primo spot next to Brooklyn and her own science journal. He couldn't blame her. Something amazing was about to happen, and he wanted in on the action. Sneaking over, he made a Brooklyn sandwich with his sister and peeked at the experiment in her book.

"Fuzzy note decoder? Just like the spy movies," he said, petting Whiplash, who slithered up his arm and onto his shoulder.

"Not quite," she said, setting up her workspace. "For this experiment, I use the actual page that needs to be decoded, not the surrounding pages." She set a funny-shaped flask directly in front of her on the table. Next to it, she slid a plastic tub full of colorful vials. "Makayla, I need you to hunt through this box and find a little blue vial with CT written on the top."

His sister squealed and started rummaging through the bin.

"I can find the vial," he said, reaching over Brooklyn to pull the tub away from his sister.

Makayla yanked the tub from his reach. "Not on your life! This is the coolest thing I've ever done. And you already have the dragon."

Whiplash screeched as if trying to prove Makayla's point. *Traitor.* Hayden picked the dragon off his shoulder and put him in his hand, enjoying the tickle of claws on his flesh. Okay, hanging out with his dragon would be better than looking for a boring vial of stuff. But he better be in on the rest of the action.

"Here. Found it!" Makayla practically threw the bottle in the air in her excitement but somehow managed to get it into Brooklyn's hands.

Brooklyn popped the lid and dumped the white powder into the glass. Hayden leaned closer, watching. Not that anything was happening yet. Everything was just—white and powdery.

"Put these on," she said, thrusting goggles into their hands. "And Makayla, get that page ready."

Goggles—things were getting real.

He slid the goggles on the top of his head the best he could with Whiplash back on his shoulder. The dragon shrieked and scrambled over his cheek, climbing up his ear. Sharp claws dug into his scalp. There was no way to get the goggles into place with a silly reptile in the way.

"Okay, I'm going to pour this liquid into the flask." Brooklyn handed tongs to Makayla. "Use these and hold the paper tight over the glass, no matter what happens."

Hayden couldn't miss this. Scooping Whiplash from his hair, he set his pet on the desk and hurried to join them. His goggles landed in place the second the liquid hit the powder.

Bubbles erupted and instantly climbed the edges of the flask. Thick purple smoke billowed from the mouth of the jar.

"Now! Hold the paper in the smoke."

Makayla kicked into action, holding the paper right above the opening. Smoke engulfed the paper until it completely disappeared behind the cloud of purple.

The smell of burnt licorice and sour gummy worms wafted over the room. Science had never smelt so good or so *strong*. He waved his hand to dissipate some of the fumes.

The experiment lasted several long Mississippi-seconds before the bubbles started to fall, and the smoke faded away.

"I forget how much smoke this makes," she said with a cough, fanning the air over the flask. "Remind me next time to half the recipe."

Next time? Awesome!

"Wow." Makayla pushed her goggles onto her frizzy hair and studied the page. "When you said 'fuzzy note decoder,' I thought you meant for fuzzy handwriting. I didn't think it would actually make *fuzzy notes*."

"Yeah, umm, about that," Brooklyn winced and took the sheet. "I tend to glitch all my science, including this experiment. So—ta-da—an actual fuzzy note."

She held the note with two fingers for them to see, an awkward smile on her face like she wasn't sure if they would be impressed or disgusted. The old brown page now had short pink hair spiking different directions—like it had mutated into a paper monster.

"Impressive." *Oops. Had he said that out loud?*

Brooklyn's awkward smile stretched. A funny feeling of satisfaction and friendship sprouted in his chest. It felt *good*. Maybe he should say stuff like that more often.

"Those are *my* gummy bears," Mr. Muffins yelped. "Get your winged demon away from my treat."

Hayden ignored Mr. Muffins's protests and brushed the soft letters with his thumb, pushing the hairs one way and then the other.

Squawk. Screeeech.

"No, you don't," Mr. Muffin yelled. "If you eat another, I'll show you how sharp my claws . . . Fine. You asked for it."

"What does it say?" Makayla asked.

Brooklyn ran a hand down the page, pushing all the fur down. Letters formed words that popped out but didn't make any sense. Except . . . *did that say "glitched dragon?"*

Meeeeeek. Screech.

"Get your dragon. It's . . ."

"I'll get you some more gummy bears," Hayden said without moving his eyes from the paper. Didn't Mr. Muffins see that they were onto something amazing over here? He could share a stinking gummy bear.

"Now!" Mr. Muffins shouted.

Hayden turned to yell at the annoying cat, but the words stuck in his throat. Instead of dark blue, Whiplash had turned the color of rotten lemons. And that wasn't all. Somehow, he'd stretched from the dark curtains, across the length of the desk, to where Mr. Muffins pinned his tail with a single, angry claw.

"What. Did. You. Do. To. Him?" Hayden said through clenched teeth. He poked Whiplash's body, and it sprung back—just like a gummy bear. Scratch that, a gummy dragon. He glared at

Mr. Muffins. Whatever science the evil cat did to hurt Whiplash, he'd be sorry.

"Don't go looking at me, big guy. I told him not to eat my gummy bear, and he did it anyhow. Seems to me that your dragon is getting what he deserves." Mr. Muffins released his claw from the tail. The whole gummy body sprung back like an overstretched rubber band. "And if he ever steals my bears again, I'll just have to see what gummy dragon tastes like."

"Mr. Muffins!" Brooklyn waved a finger at him.

The cat rolled his eyes and huffed.

"Is he broken?" Makayla asked, poking his tail. It laid overstretched and limp, like smeared Jell-O.

How could this have happened? Hayden plucked Whiplash off the curtain, his cold dragon body sticking to his fingers. "It's okay, buddy. We'll fix you." *Fix him? What even happened?*

Whiplash gagged, his body recoiling. Twisting his tail into a tight ball, he sputtered and gasped.

"He's choking," Brooklyn cried from behind him.

The room blurred into just Hayden and his dragon. He pulled Whiplash closer, not sure what to do. Would CPR save dragons? And how would he turn Whiplash back from gummy? *One thing at a time.* He rolled the little guy over, letting the soft gummy spike smoosh against his palm.

"I'm going to do CPR. Let me know if it works."

This had to work.

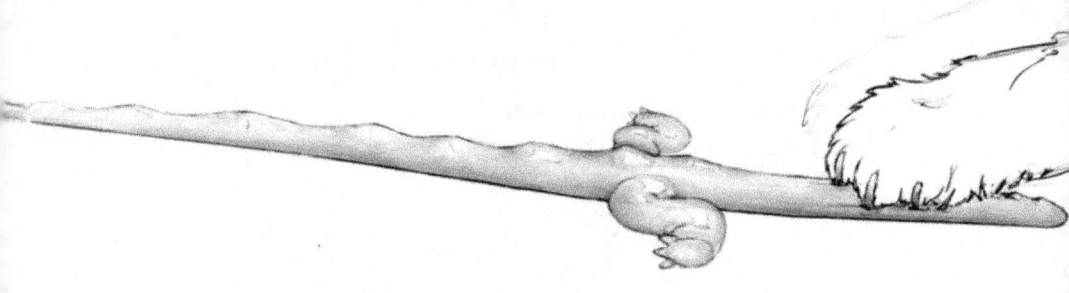

"You don't even know CPR," Makayla cried.

This was not the time for those kinds of details—he'd seen enough movies enough to know it worked. He found Whiplash's chest and pressed firmly with the tip of his finger.

The dragon opened its mouth, and a stream of yellow liquid spit out all over Hayden's cheek.

Instantly, Whiplash's scales hardened and turned dark. He rolled upright, wagged his long blue tail, and slithered up Hayden's arm. Just as fast, Hayden's face started to sizzle.

"What just happened?" Makayla asked. She waved her hands around like she was doing some crazy bat dance. "I mean, one minute he is fine, then he is the incredible-stretching gummy dude, and now everything's fine again. How is that even possible?"

"Whiplash is glitched," Brooklyn said, her head dropped. "So much for the perfect experiment going right," she added under her voice.

Glitched? The different pieces of the day started to fit together. "A food glitch," Hayden said, thinking out loud. "Spicy chips made Whiplash shoot fireballs. The punch turned him into a bottle rocket." *And made Brooklyn's room rain pink drink.* "Gummy bears made him a gummy dragon. Whatever Whiplash eats affects what happens." He fanned his face to cool down, but the burning intensified.

"Oh . . . I get it." Makayla said, plucking the dragon up and giving him a good look over. "Being glitched makes Whiplash much more fun."

"Definitely . . ." Hayden fanned his face even faster, "but guys, dragon spit feels like acid!"

"It's probably the juice," said Mr. Muffins. "These are the

juicy bears. They always have a surprise burst inside."

Since when did juice start melting flesh?

"Juice has water in it!" Brooklyn rushed around the room and brought him back a shop towel. "Here, pat it dry. Your sores are *moving*." She grimaced and thrust the towel into his hand.

Hayden pressed the towel against his cheek. Green and purple snot stuck to the white fabric and reeked of fish guts. "Hurry and read the hairy note. Or I'm going to turn into a green swamp monster!"

The Best Deal Ever
18

He was going to die. He was going to turn into a puddle of goop and die.

Hayden sank to the floor. *It's already happening.* He'd just sop into the carpet in a gooey mess. With the towel pressed firmly on his face, he waited for Brooklyn to decipher the notes. The burning slowly dissipated, but that didn't keep him from feeling like a ticking time bomb.

Brooklyn squinted at the notes. "Huh. It says we need the tears from the infectious dragon." She giggled, looking at him over the fuzzy paper. "That makes *much* more sense. Can you imagine what would happen if we just poured tears all over your face?"

Oh yeah, he could imagine. And it wasn't pretty. He'd become the Timberline Town Lizard Monster. No way Mom would let her scaly monster son inside the house. He'd have to live in the family barn, and people would pay money to see him.

At least they'd be rich.

Makayla stepped closer to Brooklyn, nearly stepping on

Hayden's hand. Well, for now, it was still a hand. What would it be when he turned into the Lizard Monster? He balled his fist and shoved it between his crossed legs.

"Tears? As in we have to make the glitched dragon cry?" Makayla asked.

"I guess," Brooklyn replied, though she didn't sound too convinced.

"But which glitched dragon? I mean, aren't both glitched?" Makayla added.

Hayden's gaze flipped to his cute little dragon. *No, not Whiplash.*

"The only two people infected are Dad and Hayden," Brooklyn said, watching Whiplash with an intense frown etched on her brow—her thinking face. "And Dad hasn't touched Whiplash. Logically, it just makes sense that it'd be the wingless dragon."

Okay, so just the lizard-thing. And they needed to make it cry.

How would they do that? Stub its toe? That always worked on him. But, somehow, he didn't think the effect would be the same. Not that it mattered. He needed to *find* the critter first.

Where would it hide?

The apple tree? Maybe. Probably—munching on yummy apples.

Makayla pointed to the fuzzy page. "What is *maida flour?* Or *nitro-ouw-whatchamacallit?*" she asked, drawing the words out.

"Different ingredients for the solution—all things Dad has in his lab," Brooklyn said in deep thought. "Which is good news. There are instructions on how to mix—evenly and only vertically. Whatever that means." She paced between them, humming her way through the list, then gasped. "Oh, no. This is bad, bad, bad."

"What is it?" Hayden asked, not sure he wanted to know.

With his current luck, the last ingredient was something you could only find in Antarctica.

"Nothing, um, *too* important. It's just," Brooklyn tapped one foot against the other, "if we don't make the antidote before—" she winced and gestured at his sores, "you turn into a dragon, there's no changing you or Dad back."

Yeah, not too important. That news slapped him upside the head.

Brooklyn sat on the floor directly across from him and gave him her serious, down-to-business stare. "I know two things. First, I need the glitched dragon to make the antidote. Second, everything else we need to make the cure is right here," she said, ticking the things off on her fingers. "You help me find the dragon-lizard. I'll start working on the cure."

Get the glitched dragon. He could do that. Doing something would beat sitting here in a puddle of self-pity.

"Take the cat with you. He's a good climber," Brooklyn said, pointing in Mr. Muffins's direction.

The feline huffed. "I don't think so. I'm still out gummy bears."

Brooklyn fisted the pencil in her hand like she was trying to strangle the thing. "This isn't a negotiation."

"Actually, it is." Mr. Muffins padded over and stood between them. "I'll help find the dragon-lizard on one condition: Whiplash goes home with him," he said with a flick of his tail in Hayden's direction. "You've made two dragons. You can make another."

Hayden's heart froze, and his eyes met Makayla's. She looked as stunned as he felt.

Brooklyn pet the top of Mr. Muffins's head, considering her options, then stopped and held out a hand to Hayden. "Deal."

Was it that easy? Should he spit on his hand before shaking like they did in movies? A spit pack was way stronger than regular ones. But she was a girl. That kind of thing probably grossed her out. Instead, he took her hand softly, not wanting to hurt her. She gripped him hard enough to snap his fingers off and show him who's boss.

So much for not wanting to hurt her. Ouch! When she let go, he slid his hand into his pocket so she wouldn't see him rubbing it against his leg.

Makayla gaped. "Really? Just like that, you'd give Whiplash up?"

He whacked his sister's ankles and hissed, "Shh." She'd mess up the whole deal.

"What?" she said, joining them on the carpet. "I just wonder, why would you do that?"

Brooklyn shrugged. "A girl never goes against her best cat. Plus, he's the best hunter in the group. Hayden will find the wingless dragon much faster with Mr. Muffins." A sly smile crossed her face. "And I can always do some science and try to make another."

"Or a unicorn?" Makayla spit out. Hayden tried not to laugh. It was amazing she'd made it this long without asking.

"Let's not get too crazy," he said. "We have some pox to cure." *And then Whiplash was his.* Now he just needed to find the glitched dragon before he became one.

Hayden ran to the apple tree with lightning speed. Sweat beaded on his forehead and melted a trail down to his back. Mr. Muffins flew past him and started climbing the tree.

Yes. Go get him.

When he reached the base of the tree, Hayden jumped and caught the lowest branch. The usually smooth bark felt like sandpaper against his burning hands. He looked up at where he grasped the branch. Big green blisters were popping out of his fingers and along his arms.

Get. The. Dragon-Lizard.

He climbed higher, hyper-aware of the moment around him—and boy, there was a lot of it! Birds fluttered in and out of the treetop, and the whole tree swayed with every inch he climbed. Even the leaves danced around, making rustling noises.

When he got to the highest branch possible for him to reach, he slumped against a branch and itched the blisters until green ooze popped and dripped between his fingers. The dragon was nowhere, vanished, invisible for all he knew.

A paw pressed into his forehead. Mr. Muffins perched above, looking down with narrowed eyes. "Giving up already?"

The feline climbed down the trunk using Hayden's head and shoulders as steps before touching down on the branch. His long fluffy tail brushed against Hayden's neck and face.

"Well, you can just go back. I'm the best hunter out of this group, and I've searched the entire tree. No dragon-lizard."

Hayden looked up at the branches swaying above him. "You've searched the entire tree?" The tree felt like it extended forever. How high did dragons climb?

"Do I look like I'm making things up?" Mr. Muffins said with a snarl. "I need to find that dragon-lizard as much as you do. If Dr. Slade morphs completely, I'm out of gummy bears and chocolate milk. A cat can't live off mice alone."

And Brooklyn wouldn't have a dad.

Hayden hadn't thought of that, but how could he when his whole body was an inferno of itching?

Don't scratch. They'll spread.

He smacked his neck—hard—like he was covered by mosquitoes. The overwhelming need to scratch stopped with each slap.

"If you were looking for someone to whack you, I'd volunteer." The cat stretched and dug his claws through the rough bark.

He glared at the cat. "I'll pass. Thanks."

"Fine, have it your way."

"If smacking myself keeps me from looking like Dr. Slade, it's worth it," Hayden said, slapping his lumpy, bumpy skin again. The sting worked for a second, but the itch came back full force.

Mr. Muffins blinked at him, then snickered. "Are you certain it's working?"

Hayden ran a hand down his face as the itch returned, times a hundred. "Nothing works. We've got to find that dragon-lizard." And it clearly wasn't sitting around in this tree waiting for them. He started down the tree, then stopped when he realized the cranky feline wasn't following. "Are you coming?"

Mr. Muffins huffed and rolled his eyes. "Humans. Always ordering me around."

"Please."

The cat stretched his body to reach a lower branch. "The boy's finally learned manners. Goody."

"Where else should we look?" Hayden asked, moving down the branch. He knew nothing about dragons, especially glitched ones. Why had the wingless beast climbed the tree to begin with?

The Best Deal Ever

He studied the twisted branches above as they waved in the breeze. Something felt off, but he couldn't put his finger on it.

What was it? He'd just climbed that tree the day before for an after-school snack.

Wait! Where were all the apples? The tree had been full of

nice red juicy ones.

Next to him, an apple hung—completely eaten to the core. *No way!* Birds pecked at the fruit on the tree all the time, leaving brown spots that looked like something had clawed at the fruit. But they never looked like this.

And the tree was full of them—apple carcasses dangling from branches and peeking out between leaves.

All dragon food. Why hadn't he thought of that before? Whiplash had the appetite of a herd of hungry hippos. That glitched dragon-lizard already finished off the apples on this tree and was headed for more.

Hayden clambered down the tree. He knew exactly where to look!

"Hey, itchy. Where are you going?" Mr. Muffins asked, following him branch for branch.

"The garden! And the last one there is a bag of rotten potatoes."

Hayden sprinted to the garden, swiped up Makayla's discarded bug cage, and planted himself between the tomatoes and the cucumbers. The garden was a jungle. Thick vines with large hairy leaves crawled across the ground, hiding everything.

The dragon-lizard could be anywhere.

"I'll search the cucumbers. You check the pumpkins," Hayden yelled at the cat.

Lifting and yanking, he pulled at the cucumber vines, finding nothing at all. No cucumbers, no flowers. How could there be nothing? Sweat dripped onto his brow and ran down his cheek. He swiped at it as fast as he could.

Pressure built on his neck, then burst. Green goop splattered across the back of his hand. It looked like lizard guts and reeked of sour pickles.

"Forget the rotten potatoes," Mr. Muffins said with an evil cackle. "It looks like you're turning into a soggy salad."

"Very funny," Hayden growled. "You find anything?"

"Your pumpkin has carved itself," he said. "There is a nice hole in one side and out the other." *Great. Makayla was going to be fuming.* "On the plus side, something ate out all the seeds."

"It's got to be here!"

Hayden turned to the tomatoes and brushed through the leaves. Only one ripe tomato hung from the vine. *So, it hadn't finished eating.*

Mr. Muffins hissed. Crouching lower, with his tail up and body ready to pounce, the cat's eyes trained on something. Hayden moved the weeds again, this time slower, watching.

In a fury of fur and whiskers, Mr. Muffins leaped past. Hayden followed on hands and knees, swooping his arms through the garden. Hard vines scraped his skin, but he squeezed his eyes shut and reached further. An unseen body wiggled against his palm. He grabbed it. The creature fought against his hold.

His eyes flew open in time to see a long green tail flicking back and forth.

"I got it!" he shouted, rushing to his knees.

Mr. Muffins padded to the edge of the garden and grabbed the bug cage with his mouth. He dropped it next to Hayden and shook his head. "Not bad. Not graceful by any means, but not bad."

Hayden brushed tomato leaves off his stomach. "What are you talking about? That was amazing. Did you even see me?"

"Yes, and I can't unsee it, unfortunately." Mr. Muffins shivered, sending fluffs of hair into the breeze. "You looked like a drowning rat."

Hayden wanted to point out that he caught the infectious dragon-lizard, and the old tabby had missed it, but then he remembered that *he* was the one turning into a dragon-thing and instantly changed his mind.

Gravel crunched from the driveway. Dad was home—another reason to hurry faster.

Swiping the bug cage and opening it with one hand, Hayden slid his other hand in but couldn't get the critter off. Every time he tried, the stinking bugger clawed him with a yellow foot.

Yellow?

He turned the cage to get a better look. Dark eyes stared back, framed by yellow scales.

Not the wingless dragon.

Defeat washed over him—defeat that felt an awful lot like dipping himself in a pot of honey and letting fire ants crawl all over him. He set the normal, non-curing lizard back in the weeds and watched it skitter off.

"Look at you, pulling weeds. Mom will be so impressed." Dad's deep voice called from the door. "Grab Makayla. It's about dinnertime."

"Just a minute, Dad."

"Make it quick," Dad said. The door shut behind him before Hayden could say anything else. Not that he had anything to say. His time was up.

And he needed help.

"Can you tell Makayla?" Hayden asked, refusing to look

at the cat. He ripped a piece of grass and threw it as hard as he could. It barely flew before landing. Just like him ... all that effort, and he was getting nowhere. "And keep looking for the dragon-lizard. I have some prep to do before dinner."

Mr. Muffins flicked his tail and took off.

Hayden hoped the cat at least pretended to help him. Because now he had more problems on his plate. Dad was home, and that meant one thing—he had two people to hide the truth from.

Mummy Hands
19

The house felt empty, but Hayden knew his parents were there—somewhere—and he didn't want to get caught. Not when he looked like he'd been slimed by a goblin with the stomach flu.

He slipped into the laundry room and rifled through Mom's first aid cabinet, grabbing anything that looked useful, then bolted to his room. He tossed his finds onto the bed, shut the door, and stripped off his shirt. Green and purple jelly-goop covered his chest where more bumps swelled, ready to burst.

Don't think about them.

Sure thing. That just made them itch more. He'd have to tell Brooklyn so she could write it in the super-secret journal for next time.

Don't let there be a next time.

Rummaging through his dresser, he found the ugly long-sleeved turtleneck Mom made him wear for their last family pictures. With the long sleeves and suffocating collar, he could cover up most of the bumps. He looked at the loot on his bed.

Three rolls of bandages laid amid random supplies—perfect for mummy hands.

Shoving the shirt over his head, he instantly remembered how tight the neck was. He'd have to force his head through.

A knock sounded at the door, and Hayden panicked with his face stuck in the neck hole. He yanked on the shirt, and his head finally popped free—just as the door slid open. Turning away from the door, he forced his arms through the sleeves.

"Mom's going to wonder if you're sick when she sees you in *that* shirt," Makayla said, a giggle hiding in her voice.

"Very funny," he said, pulling her into the room and closing the door. "It's the only thing that will cover the bumps."

In her hands, Whiplash squawked hello. Hayden rubbed a finger under the tiny dragon's chin and smiled when his pet wiggled his body in excitement.

When this was all over with, Whiplash would be his. Forever. *Unless Mom found out.*

"Are you planning on wearing gloves and a mask, too?" his sister asked with a smirk.

A mask? He ran his fingers over his face, feeling for signs of bumps. *All smooth.* His hands were another story. He swiped the bandage from his bed and tossed it at her.

Makayla set Whiplash on the floor with a tiny marshmallow. The dragon stretched his wings and started strutting around the fluffy white treat.

Hayden pushed up his sleeves and watched his sister wrap the bandage over his arm, mummy-style.

"Mr. Muffins says you caught yourself a fake dragon," she said as she worked the roll around his arm and down his wrist.

"With ninja skills he could only dream about. Too bad it was the wrong lizard." The glitched dragon-lizard had to be close by. Unfortunately, everyone on his street had fruit trees. The possibilities were endless.

She finished the knot, and he pulled the sleeve over his arm and checked out his hand. The bandage covered everything and looked super spooky—perfect.

"Don't you think Mom and Dad are going to notice you look like you escaped from the emergency room?"

"It's close to Halloween. I'll just tell them I'm checking out costume options." He handed her the other bandage. Sure, his parents would look at him like he'd lost it, but with the holiday so close, his parents would expect a little spookiness.

"Kids! Dinnertime," Mom called from downstairs.

"We'll eat dinner, then go back out and find the dragon-cure," Hayden said, fidgeting with the ends of his mummy hand. She'd messed up the end of the bandage, but he couldn't have done any better.

This was it. Showtime.

Hayden slouched in his chair, feeling exposed but trying to act natural. With Mom on one side and Dad on the other, he couldn't turn either direction without giving someone a full display of the rash growing behind his ears. He tugged the turtleneck higher but stopped messing with it when Makayla shook her head at him from across the table.

"I hear you had quite an adventure at school today," Dad said, dishing himself a heaping spoonful of mashed potatoes.

"Hayden's class was attacked by wild rats!" Makayla beamed. "The third-grade rumor is that they have nests in the walls. He was totally a hero for scaring them away."

Hayden could kiss his sister—if it weren't so *gross.*

Mom's fork clinked against the glass plate, and she coughed into her napkin. "Wild rats? That's . . . that's definitely not what I heard."

Without shifting, Hayden peeked at her from the corner of his eyes. Was she going to ask for more details? *Please, no.*

Instead, she fiddled with her plate, then started back up with dinner.

A shadow hovered over Mom's shoulder, peeking beneath her wavy hair. It stretched and moved until the light hit it just

right, and he could see dark blue scales.

Whiplash.

The dragon snaked down her sleeve, closer to the bowl of fruit salad. *What was the deal with his dragon and food?*

And how had Mom not felt him? Had his dragon somehow become *weightless?*

Wait!—Whiplash ate the marshmallow!

"How was work, Dad?" Makayla changed the subject. Having his sister on his side felt as if he had the best sidekick a superhero could ask for.

Dad stabbed a piece of lettuce. "Just a normal day at the office. Lawsuits and litigation. Nothing more exciting than yours."

He had no idea.

Whiplash poked his head out by Mom's elbow. Hayden needed a distraction. He bumped the table hard enough to rattle the dishes and reached for Mom's place. In the commotion, his cup tipped, spilling water all over—drowning his food, running along the wooden table, and covering his shirt.

The instant the ice-cold water touched his skin, it sizzled. He screamed and stood, sending his chair tumbling to the floor.

"Calm down. It's just an accident," Mom said, throwing her napkin on top of the puddle gathering in the middle of the table.

Hayden's chest felt like worms wiggled and slid under his skin. Everything ached, tickled, and jiggled. Bits of him exploded under his clothes, and goopy lava oozed down his stomach. He felt like he might just throw up all over Mom and his dinner.

He gagged, coughed, and choked the urge down. Over Mom's head, Makayla waved her hands frantically. *What now?* She pointed to her chin and then his.

No! He traced the edges of three large bumps and the hint of several smaller beneath his skin at his chin. Pulling the turtleneck up and over his mouth like a face mask, he backed up. He'd go to his room and hide until he was eighty. Mom would never notice. In fact, with all the messes he'd caused, she might be happier.

As he turned to leave, he spotted Whiplash racing down Mom's back. He snagged his dragon and held him against his stomach, then speed-walked out of the room.

"Hayden looks sick," Makayla said behind him as he slipped around the corner.

He'd do her chores and then some for all the times she'd saved him today—assuming he didn't completely change into the lizard man first.

Hayden rushed into his room and shut the door, leaving him in a gray darkness. Dragon pox covered his ears, tickled his neck, climbed his stomach, and now speckled his face. And the water burned like acid.

There was a knock on his door.

"Hayden?" Mom said through the wood.

Whiplash fidgeted against his grip, and the door handle shook. "Hayden?"

He slid down the door to the floor, releasing Whiplash. The dragon waddled under the desk to a pile of crumbs.

The knob shook again. There was no way she'd go away until he answered.

"I have something for you," she said.

He scooted forward, and the door opened a crack. It was the moment of truth because there was no way he could keep up with the lies any longer.

Antidote

20

Hayden sat in the dark room, leaning against the door and wishing he could disappear. Mom sat in the hallway, the door between them. Sure, it was only inches apart, but it felt like they were miles.

"I liked your ninja-mummy look at dinner," she said through the cracked doorway.

He rubbed his hands on his jeans, the bandages rolling together with the friction. "Thanks."

Her taps on the wooden door made a ticking sound. "I thought you hated that shirt," she said, like she was grasping at any conversation. She didn't have to. He'd rather just be alone. "It's kind of nice to see you wear it again, even if it's for dress-up."

More like cover-up. "Yeah." His mouth only allowed the lame one-word answers. Inside, Hayden felt more terrible than he ever had in his whole life.

Whiplash strutted across the floor near him, completely unaware of what Hayden was feeling.

No one cared.

"Do you want to talk about whatever is bothering you?" Mom asked.

Talk about it? What could he say? *I hate the no-pet rule, so I tried to catch my own, but instead, I caught the dragon pox. If I don't find that stinking dragon-lizard again, I'm going to turn into Lizard Boy.* Yeah, right.

Hayden groaned a "na-ah."

"So, look. I know you've wanted a pet for a long time," Mom said. "Maybe we've both been going about this the wrong way."

His heart began to squeeze. *She knows I'm lying.*

"I've been thinking," Mom continued, her voice soft—way too soft to be explosive at him for sneaking a pet. Still, he braced himself for what was coming next. "I've been against having a pet in the house because I've been certain I'd end up being the one taking care of it. But maybe it's time for me to give you a chance to prove yourself."

His muscles relaxed. She *wasn't* mad. Then . . . *what?*

A mason jar with a cloth top slid through the door next to him. Several twigs bunched together in the jar, and on top of the thickest stick laid a puke green lizard. It flicked its tongue—neon orange. Hayden grabbed the jar and pulled it closer to his face. The lizard blinked back.

Not a lizard—the wingless dragon!

She'd found the cure. He could be saved.

Whiplash hissed and scrambled backward, away from the jar, then darted under a pile of dirty pajamas. The dragon-lizard in the jar only blinked again.

"You wouldn't believe where I found this guy." She chuckled.

"I was digging up potatoes in the garden, and the lizard ran across my feet and up my leg—under my pants! I bet I looked ridiculous trying to get him out. But when he turned out to be so unique and interesting—just like you—I figured, why not?"

Hayden pictured Mom dancing around the garden, screaming and shaking her leg. Or, maybe she didn't scream. She wasn't like Mrs. Bowers, jumping onto the desk and filing cabinet.

"We will have to get a bigger cage. And it will be *your* responsibility to take care of him."

A tear slid down his cheek, and he swiped at it before it could do any damage. "Thanks, Mom. I will. I promise." He set the jar beside him, scooted, and opened the door just enough to circle her in his arms.

He'd finally got what he wanted, but it wasn't what he thought—not a pet. Trust.

She reached around the door and wrapped him into a tight hug. A horrible guilt monster squeezed at his stomach. She trusted him, and he was lying to her.

"What are you going to name it?" Her words tickled his hair. She released him and picked up the jar. "Maybe something like Turbo, because this little dude is lightning fast when he wants to be." She tapped her fingernail against the glass. The creature didn't budge. "Or Potato, because now he's acting like a couch potato on a log."

He loved it when she was goofy like this. Hayden shifted to lean against the door frame, closer to Mom.

"Potato is a silly name for a pet," he said with a laugh. He looked from the jar to her hand clutching it, and to the large bump growing on her thumb. The ugly bump stared at him.

Mom had the pox!

"I . . . I'm going to name it Antidote," he said. *And get the dragon-lizard to Brooklyn as fast as I can.* Brooklyn had the book. She could save Mom.

"Antidote? That's an interesting name," Mom said, opening the jar and pulling Antidote out. She turned him side to side. "I guess it fits." She handed him to Hayden, then rubbed his hair and pulled him in for another hug.

A big fat juicy blister on his neck exploded. He tensed. Mom flinched.

"Good gracious, I think he peed on me. And it smells like

rotten fish sticks," she said, pinching her nose and scooting away. "Maybe you should have named that guy Stinky Pickles."

Hayden fake chuckled. If only she knew what was really on her shirt.

She shook the green stain on her sleeve and stood. "I'll let you two settle in," she said, then headed down the hall and into her room.

He needed to save her—now.

And now he could.

Bathwater started roaring from the master bathroom.

Mom's tub!

NO ITCHING AND NO WATER.

Hayden slipped Antidote in the jar and tripped over himself to get to his feet. He had to stop her, but his parent's door shut before he could reach it.

He knocked, but she didn't answer. Panic raced over every bump on his skin. Sprinting to his room, he snatched Antidote and started down the stairs.

Wait, he couldn't leave Whiplash!

He raced back, threw the pajamas aside, and caught the hidden dragon. The sound of rushing water taunted him as he ran back to the hall. Hayden flew down the stairs and nearly ran over Makayla at the bottom.

"Guess what? Dad's watching that law show, and Mom's in the bath. We can head over to Brooklyn's," Makayla said, fling her unicorn backpack over her shoulder and reaching for the door. She stopped when she looked back at him. "Oh! You found the dragon-lizard. Where was—"

"I need you to stall Mom's bath!" he shouted at her.

"Why would I do that?" Makayla asked. "She'll be busy for hours."

"She has the pox."

"Oh, Unicorn Tails!" Makayla stumbled back a step and dropped the backpack from her shoulder. "You *are* contagious." She pulled up her sleeves and studied her freckly arms.

"I'm not contagious." Hayden lifted the jar. "He is." Antidote flicked out his tongue and tore a piece of bark, then swallowed it whole. His scales flickered brown, then back to green. "Mom caught him and the pox. I've got to get the cure, and you've got to save her."

He slipped through the door, peeking his head in one last time. "Remember. No baths. You have to stop her at all costs!"

Makayla started to the kitchen like she had time for a snack before stopping Mom.

"Where are you going?" He asked in disbelief. "Mom's upstairs!"

Makayla rolled her eyes and smirked. "Amateur. I've got this."

Crisp air bit at Hayden as he booked it to Brooklyn's house. The house hid in the darkness of the night, with only a few lights in windows to prove someone was home.

He didn't know if he should knock or not. In the movies, boys tossed pebbles at their friends' windows, but with his luck, he'd probably shatter the glass and end up in a ton of trouble.

"Interesting time for a visit," a sarcastic voice sounded from the bush.

The Slades had talking bushes now? No way did he want to

find out what else it said. Setting the jar on the step, he raised a fist to knock.

"I wouldn't do that if I were you," the bush said. "Dr. Slade might answer."

He paused, fist mid-swing. "What am I supposed to do then?"

The bush jostled, and Mr. Muffins stalked out from under thick leaves. The feline began climbing the shrubbery to the window above. "Wait for Brooklyn."

Fizz and Pop

21

Long fluorescent bulbs buzzed to life, shining light throughout the giant barn-lab. The tables that lined the enormous space were filled with glowing solutions and bubbling concoctions. Hayden instinctively glanced to the back corner. The dragon incubator sat charred and abandoned.

Brooklyn laid the old leather book and a glass of brown mixture—*the start of the cure?*—on the work table. Hayden pulled the turtleneck down from his face to get a better look.

"Man, you look like a swamp monster," Brooklyn said with a grimace. Considering how much popping and oozing was happening, he might as well be one.

"We've got trouble. Like *big trouble,*" he said, setting Whiplash and the jar with Antidote on the table next to the book. "My mom has the dragon pox, and she's about to take a bath."

"Talk about an explosive way for her to find out she's infected," Mr. Muffins said as he jumped onto the table. He padded across the book, hissed at Whiplash, and lapped up some of the brown potion.

Hayden cringed. There was no way he'd drink that potion after the cat's tongue touched it. A sore on his face burst, splatting thick muck in his eye.

Correction: He'd drink whatever Brooklyn gave him.

"Seriously, Mr. Muffins. You're slopping your chocolate milk all over." Brooklyn pushed her feline off the book and snatched it up. "Whoever says cats are cleaner pets hasn't met this one."

Chocolate milk—not the cure. That was a relief.

The lab door burst open, and someone—or some*thing*—staggered in. He wore clothes that looked like Dr. Slade's, but green scales covered his face instead of skin. Hayden clutched the counter for safety from . . . the *Lizardinator*.

"Dad!" Brooklyn dropped the book and ran to the Lizardinator.

Hayden narrowed his eyes and studied the thing in the doorway. *That* was Dr. Slade.

"I'm sorry, Dad. I'm going to save you," Brooklyn cried, guiding her dad to a chair against the wall. The doc staggered and tripped, like he didn't know how to use his legs anymore. Maybe he didn't. They were human legs, after all, and not much about him looked human anymore.

Dr. Slade slid from the chair and started crawling on the floor on all fours—like a hybrid alligator.

That kicked Hayden into gear. "Mom!" She'd finally trusted him with an animal, and now she might turn into one.

Brooklyn opened the leather book with hands so shaky that she almost dropped it twice. Her finger ran down the fuzzy page taped back into the book, then slowed over the word "dragon."

"We can do this . . . Hopefully." Her voice sounded uncertain and scared, but she stood taller and started moving flasks around the table. "I've actually done most of the experiment while you were searching for the dragon-lizard." She motioned to a vial of cloudy purple liquid. "We just need to add one ingredient."

"The last ingredient, check." Hayden lifted the jar and watched Antidote climb the glass wall of his jail cell.

"Right. Dragon tears," she said, pulling the corner of her lips down. "We'll have to make it cry."

"How do we do that," he asked. The idea of hurting Antidote made his skin crawl and his bumps burn. It didn't matter that the scaly guy caused him all this pain. He couldn't hurt it back.

Mr. Muffins stopped lapping the chocolate milk and licked his chops. "I'm sure I could help make that thing cry." He ran his tongue over one long white fang, then grinned.

Hayden was done with the cranky cat and his jabs. He grabbed the jar to protect his lizard-dragon pet. "Eat Antidote," he started, glaring at the feline, "and you'll turn into the world's fuzziest lizard."

The tabby didn't look amused. "At least I'm not the one with gills," Mr. Muffins said, wagging an eyebrow.

Gills? Hayden grabbed at his neck. Just below his jaw, his skin stopped, and cold, slick scales started.

It was happening. And Mom was next.

The scales suddenly felt tight, choking him. The room started to whirl around him, and he leaned against the table to keep from falling.

Brooklyn nabbed the jar out of his hand before he dropped it. "Antidote. Perfect name. Though you could easily have named him Virus." She unscrewed the lid and picked up a squirming

Antidote with a long pair of forceps.

"Another animal with a better name," Mr. Muffins grumbled under his breath. The cat scowled, then something else caught his attention. "You've got to be kidding me. Your fire-breathing devil is drinking my chocolate milk."

"We don't have time for all your food complaints," Hayden hissed. Was it too late to lock the cat back in the bush?

Whiplash hung from its tail into the glass and smiled back at Mr. Muffins, a chocolate mustache across its dragon lips.

"Oh, I don't think so." Mr. Muffins leaped at the glass. Hayden grabbed the angry cat just in time before the beast knocked the cup over and made everything worse.

Mr. Muffins clawed at Hayden's arms, slicing against his already sore skin. *That gash was all the stinking cat's fault to begin with.* He shifted the grouch around in his arms, but the tip of his soft tail brushed against his face—tickling the skin between his mouth and nose. The sensation almost made him cry.

"Wait. We don't have to hurt Antidote," Hayden yelled. Mr. Muffins stopped fighting against his hold and shot him an annoyed look. "We can tickle him!"

"That's perfect," Brooklyn said, holding Antidote in the air. The dragon-lizard struggled against the metal tools.

A metal tray crashed against the concrete in the corner of the room. Brooklyn sucked in air as her monster-dad scampered around the floor. *Was that a tail poking out from the back of his pants?* The man's hands still looked human, but that was about it.

"Hurry, what do we tickle him with?" she yelled in full panic mode, waving Antidote around.

Hayden grabbed ahold of Mr. Muffins's poof. "His tail."

"You have *got* to be joking," the cat growled. "It's always Mr. Muffins this, and Mr. Muffins that. No one cares what *I* want."

"I have a package of gummy bears with your name on it when this is over," Hayden said. He'd figure out how to make good on that promise when Dr. Slade was human again.

"Fine. But you owe me a whole factory of gummy bears when this is over," Mr. Muffins grumbled.

"You hold the lizard," Brooklyn said, holding the handle side of the forceps out to him. "Mr. Muffins, you tickle him. I'll get the tears."

The second Hayden took the forceps from Brooklyn, something hard slammed into his legs. Hayden fell into the table, knocking into the glass of chocolate milk, but catching it before it spilled.

"Dad, stop! We're trying to save you."

Dr. Slade jammed into Hayden again, almost pulling him down. He dropped the forceps. Antidote was free.

Brooklyn pushed her dad away as Hayden struggled to catch the dragon-lizard. He dove at the lizard, catching it with cupped hands. Then he peeked in. With lightning speed, Antidote scrambled free through the small hole and launched himself at Brooklyn. She screamed and jumped out of the infected dragon's way.

Mr. Muffins pounced but missed.

Burrrrrrp!

A milk bubble shaped like a large balloon floated free from Whiplash's scaly mouth. Antidote collided with the giant bubble. Instead of popping, the bubble-balloon sucked the dragon-lizard inside, trapping it in the bubble-balloon and lifting it helpless in the air.

Hayden grabbed his chest, where his heart raced in circles.

"Holy flipper skippers. I thought we lost him for good."

"And I thought I was next," Brooklyn said with a shaky voice.

He plucked the milk bubble from the air. Antidote crawled around the sides and upside down in the bubble cage. "Looks like Whiplash's glitch might have saved the day."

The chocolate milk bubble burst, splashing cold milky liquid over Hayden's cheeks and neck. A new eruption of pus and goop splattered from his face and onto his arms. Somewhere next to him, Hayden heard Brooklyn gasp and the cat gag.

Get the tears now or turn into a dragon.

Without a second thought, he grabbed Mr. Muffins's tail. The cat hissed and scrambled, but Hayden's grip was tighter.

"Laugh, little buddy," he said, grazing Antidote's tummy with the tip of the hairs of the long fluffy tail. Green scales changed to a lemony yellow. He moved the tail faster and faster. Suddenly, Antidote squealed in what could only be lizard laughter.

One thick golden tear ran down and dripped into the solution Brooklyn held. "Get more. Just in case," she said, swirling the liquid together.

Blisters on Hayden's hands sizzled and exploded.

Mr. Muffins's eyes grew. "Don't touch me with those. I'll do the rest."

About time.

Frantically, the cat wiggled the end of his tail. Antidote squawked and huffed. Three more plump tears fell from his eyes.

The purple chemical antidote in Brooklyn's hand turned tropical punch red. "Got it!"

Dr. Slade moaned and tipped over with a thump.

We're going to save you!

The doc squirmed and moaned but didn't get back up.

"I can't do it," Brooklyn cried. "What if this solution is glitched? I could kill him."

"If you don't, he's not exactly going to be enjoying human life," Mr. Muffins huffed.

Hayden watched the Lizardinator on the ground. Scales covered his hands, but there were still fingers. There was still a human in there. *For now.*

"I'll drink it," he said, sounding braver than he felt.

Brooklyn pinched her lips together. "It could glitch you, too."

He shook his head. "It'll be fine. I believe in you."

She hesitated, but then poured some of the mixture into a tiny medicine cup. "Are you sure?"

As sure as possible.

He stuffed Antidote back into his jar and tightened it up before grabbing the cup. If this didn't work, he would be the incredible lizard boy forever. And Mom? Well, that was a whole different level of bad.

He stared at the fizzy liquid, hoping it didn't taste as bad as it looked. If this worked, the rash would be gone, and he could cure Mom.

And if the experiment glitched . . . he didn't want to think about what new *thing* he'd end up with. Squeezing his eyes shut, Hayden tipped the cup and gulped.

Forget tropical punch. The solution tasted like sweetened dragon vomit. He drew a hand to his face to check for lumps and brought it back wet with thick ooze. The bursting intensified until it felt like his face was covered with pop rocks.

"It's worse!" Brooklyn cried, then started skimming the instructions and muttering to herself. "Stir vertically. We forgot to stir vertically."

The fizzing intensified, and he began to swell up. "What do I do?" he mumbled through bloated lips.

"Jump up and down," Mr. Muffins yelled. "Before you explode for real."

He was going to die! *All because he had to touch that evil lizard.*

Hayden started bouncing, ponging on one foot then the other. With each jump, he swelled bigger and bigger.

"He's going to blow!" Mr. Muffins screamed, taking cover behind a stack of books.

Brooklyn ran frantically from table to table, looking through different potions and chemicals. "I never should have let you drink that. I should have known it wouldn't work," she said, grabbing bottles and vials. "Please don't die."

He kept hopping, his head feeling lighter and lighter. *I am going to die.*

POP!

Yep. I died.

The room filled with minty foam, sizzling like liquid rockets, and Hayden collapsed to the ground.

Glass crashed. "Hayden!" Footsteps raced toward him, and Brooklyn started batting the marshmallow foam off his face. "I'm so sorry. It's all my fault."

I'm not dead.

He sat up and shoved the rest of the gunk from his face. "Did it get worse?"

Brooklyn launched herself at him, squeezing him breathless.

"Well. That was . . . unexpected," Mr. Muffins said, and he and Whiplash looked down from the edge of the table. Foam dripped from the cat's ears, and Whiplash licked it away.

"But did it work?" Or had he turned into something worse? Hayden pulled himself from his friend's grasp and really ran his hands down his face.

Nothing.

Nothing but smooth skin.

He hooted, grabbing Brooklyn into his own tight squeeze. Cured! He was cured.

But the others. Somewhere under all the puffy foam, Dr. Slade was seconds away from the point of no return.

"Hurry! Split the antidote. You need to save your dad, and I need to help my mom!" Hayden waded through the foam and grabbed the flask while Brooklyn clinked around in the cupboards.

She poured some of the fizzing liquid into a small jar and handed it to Hayden. "Good luck."

"And don't forget your demon dragon," Mr. Muffins added.

Hayden nodded and slipped Whiplash onto his shoulder. The Lizardinator groaned and rolled on the ground near the door. Seeing Dr. Slade in so much pain was scarier than the scales and lizard face. "Do you need my help?"

"I've got Mr. Muffins," she said, pushing him to the door. "We can do this. Go save your mom!"

She was right. He'd been gone for eternity. Long enough for the worst to happen. Hayden waved the small jar once, then sped through the door.

Time for the Truth
22

Hayden charged through the front door of his house, gripping the jar so tight that his fingerprints were probably embedded into the glass.

"What took you so long?" Makayla called from the top of the stairs.

Securing Whiplash with a hand on his shoulder, he raced up two at a time. "It's not easy to get dragon tears." *Or to explode into a foaming mess.*

She jabbed a finger in the direction of their parent's door. "No. What's not easy is keeping Mom out of a bath once she has her mind set on it. I had to use drastic measures. Do you know *how* much oatmeal it takes to fill a bathtub?"

Oatmeal? Makayla won the award for best covert missions.

"Or how hard it was to clean the oatmeal back out again once I got caught?" she added.

He handed her the cure, cutting her off. "We need to shake this up and down and get her to drink it." He winced, remembering what happened when *he* drank the stuff. "But, it might be messy."

Very messy.

Makayla knocked on Mom's door before they could come up with a plan.

Dad cracked the door open. From somewhere behind it, Hayden could hear Mom rant about the oatmeal.

"I know she was trying to help, but seriously? What was she thinking? Five cartons of oatmeal! And don't even get me started on this ointment. It's supposed to calm the itching, but this rash just keeps getting worse. Where is that ridiculous backscratcher your mother gave us for Christmas last year?"

"Hey, guys. This might not be the best time," Dad whispered and ducked when Mom threw a tube across the room.

"We need Mom," Makayla said.

"That's a negative Ghost Rider. She's . . . unavailable." His voice was soft, but even he looked scared.

"Please. It's important," Hayden pleaded. *So important.* Dad didn't budge. How would he get him to understand? He needed to tell the truth. Only one thing could come close to this. "This is Tiger-shredding-the-curtains kind of important. I *need* to talk to Mom."

Dad's eyes bulged from his face, but he stepped aside. Hayden swallowed the lump in his throat. This was it.

Water roared in the bathroom next to them, filling the tub. One drop of that water would multiply the problem, let alone the entire bath.

Mom stood in a bathrobe and stared into the mirror. "You have to be kidding me." She pulled at her skin around the sore, now forming on her cheeks. Hayden's stomach was going to tie itself into a permanent knot.

"Hey, Mom," he whispered, then paused—realizing that he wasn't exactly sure where to start or what to say. Whiplash shifted under his grip.

Time for the truth.

But if he told her the truth, he might lose Whiplash forever.

She ignored him, rubbing vigorously at a green welt on her neck. Saving Mom was much more important than keeping Whiplash.

"There's something I need to show you."

She turned from the mirror. Besides the polka-dots, Mom's face paled, and her lips sank. She fell onto the edge of her bed, defeated. "What is it, Hayden?"

Makayla tiptoed next to the bed with the cure punch in her hand. Could he just hand her the drink and run? Sure. But that wouldn't fix this, not all the way.

"Please, whatever you do . . . don't freak out," he said, then he pulled Whiplash off his shoulder and cupped him between his hands. "Remember how you said truth and trust were the most important things? I understand that now."

Mom gave a confused nod.

"I need you to trust me." *Even if I don't deserve it.* He uncurled his hands. Whiplash stretched his head and unfolded his wings.

Mom threw a hand to her lips but didn't scream. *Well, that's something.*

He'd made it this far—might as well tell her everything. "This is Whiplash. It wasn't a rat loose at school, it was this guy, and it was totally an accident. And he . . ." His eyes teared up, "he's my friend."

Whiplash circled Hayden's palm, giving Mom a full show of the swirls decorating its back, then sneezed snot all over his skin. She flinched, finally dropping her hand. Her eyes watching the dragon.

The bathwater stopped, and Dad's heavy hand rested on Hayden's back. "Honey, your bath's ready. But . . ." He leaned closer to Whiplash. The dragon beat his wings and squawked. "Wait, is that a *dragon?*"

Makayla chuckled and nodded. "Yes, Hayden's pet dragon. He's still a baby."

Dad held out a finger for Whiplash to climb onto but pulled it away before the dragon could latch on. "How is this even possible? Are there more?"

"About that . . ." Hayden winced. "Okay, so, there's another dragon. But it's glitchy, and it may or may not have given you dragon pox." He flashed her an innocent smile, but it dropped into a grimace as the blister on Mom's cheek grew larger.

Mom shook her head and blinked her eyes. "Dragon . . . what?"

"Dragon pox," Makayla said. "Hayden had it, and it almost turned him into a dragon."

Mom gasped and threw her hands to her face.

"Makayla!" He couldn't believe she told.

"What?" She shrugged. "It's not like we aren't planning on saving her. That *is* the plan, right?" She dangled the glass jar haphazardly by the lid with two fingers.

Of course, it was the plan, but she didn't have to go and tell all the worst parts.

"I think maybe you should explain," Dad said, crossing his arms and shaking his head.

"The lizard Mom caught me is actually a glitched dragon," Hayden confessed. All this telling the truth stuff was getting easier and easier. "I tried to catch it yesterday and ended up infected. And well, Mom touched it today."

Mom scratched at the purple welts on her cheek. One burst, spraying jelly goop. She swiped the sore with her hand, then screamed and flailed her hands. Everything was way more gross and terrifying when he watched it happen to Mom.

"But we can fix it. Look." He dumped Whiplash into one hand and used the other to pull down on his turtleneck. "See. My bumps are gone."

Her fingers traced over his skin where the blisters once swelled.

"All you have to do is drink this," Makayla added, thrusting the bottle at their mom.

She looked skeptically at the liquid, took a whiff, and pushed it away. "I don't know what's in this, but there's no way I'm drinking that."

"It's all about trust, right?" Hayden said and held the bottle back to her. "Trust me. You *need* to drink this."

Mom hesitated for way too long.

"Please." He shook the potion. "Just try it."

She took it, closed her eyes, and sighed, then brought it up to her lips.

"Wait!" He yelled.

Her eyes flew open. "What?"

"I forgot, you need to shake the jar up and down. It's kind of important."

Covering the opening with the cork, Mom shook the mixture up and down. With each shake, the bright liquid faded. She stopped and held out the potion.

Makayla covered her hands on Mom's and started shaking. "Keep shaking!"

She shook faster until the liquid was completely clear.

"This is the coolest thing I've seen today," Dad said. Whiplash huffed and blew out a puff of smoke. "Sorry. I mean the second coolest thing."

Mom opened the jar and raised it to her lips. Then she

threw it back and gulped. Hayden winced, remembering the awful taste—like dragon armpits—but Mom smacked her lips.

She pulled the cup from her mouth and inspected the liquid. "Yum. Lemon-lime, my favorite." *What? And he got the armpit version?*

Pop! Pop, pop, pop!

One by one, each of her blisters exploded. Instead of goop or foam, they burst into soap bubbles that filled the air and floated around them. She rushed to the mirror, a flurry of bubbles following her.

"How in the world?" She rubbed her fingers over her forehead. "My skin is back to new."

Hayden jumped at her, wrapping his one free arm around her waist. She pulled him closer in a tight hug, then another arm wrapped around him—Makayla's.

"Family hug." Dad joined on the other side, turning them into a hug-burrito.

Whiplash shrieked, sounding more like a duck than a dragon.

Mom jumped. "I'm not sure about this." She released Hayden and studied Whiplash. "This thing can't give me dragon pox. Can it?"

"If Whiplash were infectious, I'd be covered with pox from head to toe," Makayla laughed, plucking Whiplash out of Hayden's hand and rubbing his scaly face against her cheek. He purred and stuck out his long blue tongue.

Hayden would never admit it out loud, but without his sister, the day would have been a total disaster.

"I don't know, honey, I think he's a keeper," said Dad, holding his hand out. Makayla set Whiplash into it, and he scurried along

Dad's arm to his elbow, then squawked, turned, and slithered back to his palm.

Mom ran a hesitant finger along Whiplash's tiny head. "Look. I'm glad you came clean."

Hayden gave her his biggest, pleading smile.

Shaking her head, she sighed. "Fine. But we have more to talk about in the morning."

He could keep him. Whiplash could stay, and Hayden didn't have to keep any secrets.

That night, Hayden laid in bed, glow-in-the-dark stars on his ceiling twinkling above him. Mom had arranged them in constellations across the "sky," except for a group that spelled a simple "hi." All this time, he'd thought she was the enemy, always saying no. Really, he'd been his own enemy all along.

Whiplash curled next to him on a pillow, its tongue buzzing as it snored.

Everything was so much lighter now, like a tower of jumbo bricks had fallen off his shoulders. He didn't have to hide anything anymore.

Hayden tucked the doll blanket Makayla loaned him around Whiplash's feet and tail. Yes, everything was going to be good from now on.

It Ended With a Friend
23

The heat of the midday sun beat the top of Hayden's head as he camped out in the middle of the garden. Sweat rolled down his cheek, and he brushed it away with his hands.

"You got a little mud right about here." Brooklyn's teasing voice was a welcomed change to his boring, chore-filled day. Turned out, Mom would let him keep Whiplash, but she wasn't too keen on him sneaking the dragon to school. She and Dad decided a day of extra helping around the house might remind him about the no pets at school rule.

Hayden stood and wiped both hands on his legs. Brooklyn laughed, pointing at his pants. "Now you have mud everywhere. Bet your mom is going to love that."

He shrugged, glancing down at the finger-thick dirt striped across his pants. "If you think that's bad, you should see this." He turned, showing her the gigantic brown stain covering his entire hind end.

She giggled and shook her head at him. "Nice."

"Oh look, the kid has soiled himself." The old tabby popped out from under the pumpkin leaves.

Hayden brushed the dirt from his rear. "Have not."

Brooklyn shot Mr. Muffins a stern look, but the cat only sauntered to the fence and made himself comfortable on the post.

"How'd everything go in the lab?" Hayden asked, dumping a pile of weeds into a large bucket and fluffing them a bit so it looked full. "How's your dad?"

She beamed. "No scales or tails. Your mom?"

"Same." *Had he grown a tail?* He swiped at his pants one more time, feeling for any sign of growth.

None. Good.

"Are you going to show him, or were we just coming over to *talk?*" Mr. Muffins hocked up the last word like it were a hairball.

And the cat thought *Hayden* was the crazy one.

Brooklyn pulled a paper from her pocket and unfolded it. "Timberline Science Club. Where Science Comes to Play" was printed on the top with bold letters.

"Dad thinks I should join. Says it's a good place to make friends and show off my skills." Brooklyn shrugged and started to refold the paper. "But I don't know. I'll probably glitch it up."

He nudged her with his elbow, the only part of him that wouldn't leave a mud print. "You should do it."

She avoided his gaze, staring at the flyer. "I don't know. What if I fail? Again. Last night's success could have been a fluke."

Whiplash squawked from where he sat next to the bucket of weeds.

"What if you don't?" Hayden said, nodding towards his pet dragon.

Brooklyn opened the flyer again, reading the words as if they were new. "What do you think, Mr. Muffins?"

"I think it's time for you to show the world who's boss."

For once, Hayden and the cat agreed on something.

She waved the page between them, a spark of excitement flashing in her eyes. "How about we join the science club together."

He glanced past her to the barn-lab where everything started. Was he willing to play around in the lab again? A half-smile pulled at his lips. *Absolutely.*

Mr. Muffins pointed a freshly sharpened claw at Hayden. "Just make sure you keep that fire-breathing monster at home. And don't forget the gummy bears."

COMING SOON . . .

DITCH THE GLITCH

Science is life!

At least, that's what Brooklyn Slade thought. But after a misfortunate incident forces her to leave the Institute of Extraordinary Science and transfer to Timberline Elementary, she isn't so sure.

Atoms!

Everyone at her new school seems so *boring*. Where are the student chemists, biologists, or inventors?

When Dad tells her about the science club's Humans vs. Zombies meeting, Brooklyn decides the best way to make new friends is to wow them with a science creation—zombie flowers. Only, something glitches—again—turning them into a chomping Snapdragon Monster!

Why does this *keep* happening?

Brooklyn is beginning to question if it's her science that's glitched . . . or her.

Want more insightful, empowering, fun children's books?
Want activities and links to go along with the story?
Visit us at www.lawleypublishing.com

For updates and info on New Releases follow us at

lawleypublishing

@kidsbookswithheart

LAWLEY PUBLISHING

Camille lives in Utah with her fantastic husband, four energetic kids, and a clever fish named Holly. She loves writing adventure stories, where the 'happily ever after' only happens after things get really crazy, and the good guy always wins. When she isn't writing (or reading), Camille is a self-proclaimed science geek—who has only rarely endangered her kids with all their awesome science experiments—and a civil engineer, working locally to help rural communities around the state.

Camille is a member of the League of Utah Writers and the America Night Writers Association.
Find her at:
http://camillesmithsonauthor.com/.
Instagram: @camille_smithson_author
Facebook: @camillesmithsonauthor
Pinterest: @camillesmithsonwrites

Shareen was born in Salt Lake City, Utah, and found her love for art at an early age. They say that if you want a child to learn to read, then read with them—the same works for art. Shareen's passion was ignited at the age of two from her mom, who would sit down and color in coloring books with her. She and her hubby now live in Texas with her five kids, three cats, and one dog. When Shareen is not busy with art and empowering her family, she explores new places, learns new things, and occasionally writes poetry.

CPSIA information can be obtained
at www.ICGtesting.com
Printed in the USA
LVHW081510080722
723062LV00005B/490